Bones

Bones

Bill Pronzini

PaperJacks LTD.

TORONTO   NEW YORK

PaperJacks

BONES

PaperJacks LTD.

330 STEELCASE RD. E., MARKHAM, ONT. L3R 2M1
210 FIFTH AVE., NEW YORK, N.Y. 10010

St. Martin's Press edition published 1985

PaperJacks edition published November 1986

ISBN 0-7701-0451-7
Printed in Canada

For Ed McBain, a name to be reckoned with in the detective field—a novel about a detective in the field who reckons without a name

My love, she sleeps! Oh, may her sleep
As it is lasting, so be deep!
Soft may the worms about her creep!
—Edgar Allan Poe
The Sleeper

The evil that men do lives after them;
The good is oft interred with their bones.
—Shakespeare
Julius Caesar

Bones

ONE

The house was in one of San Francisco's secluded residential neighborhoods, so neatly tucked away on top of a hill that most of the city's inhabitants would have had to consult a map to find it. I hadn't needed a map, but that was only because I had received explicit directions from the owner of the house, a man named Michael Kiskadon, who wanted to hire me. He had been vague about what he wanted to hire me to do—"It's not something I can explain very easily on the phone," he'd said. Then he'd said, "But I can guarantee it's a job you'll find interesting, one you're well suited for. Can you come here so we can talk? I've had some medical problems and my doctor keeps me housebound these days."

So here I was, up at the top of Twelfth Avenue across from Golden Gate Heights Park. It was eleven o'clock on a Monday morning, the sun was shining, there wasn't much wind—all in all, a pleasant October day—but hardly anybody was out on the tennis courts or the children's playground or on the wide green that paralleled the street for more than a block. It was a nice park, with big trees and picnic facilities and woody hillside paths; and from its west end you would have a sweeping view of the ocean. But its seclusion probably meant it was used more or less exclusively by the people in the neighborhood. Lucky for them, too bad for everybody else.

Not that this was a particularly affluent area. The houses lining the uphill curve of Twelfth Avenue to the east, and those back down the hill on Cragmont, were middle-class and well kept up, but mostly plain and on the smallish side. The one I wanted was opposite the park green—a semi-detached

1

place that resembled a cottage more than anything else. It was painted blue. Behind a picket fence was a yard full of shrubs and acid-blue hydrangeas and a walkway that blended into a covered side porch.

I parked next to the green and got out. The air smelled of bay laurel, which is a good spicy smell, and I found myself smiling a little as I crossed the street. I was in pretty high spirits today, for no reason other than the balmy weather and maybe the fact that Kerry and I had spent the night together, doing what people do when they spend the night together. Kerry is my lady and a joy to be with, in or out of bed—most of the time, anyway. This morning I loved her even more than usual. This morning I loved everybody, even my partner Eberhardt and his stupid blond fiancée, Wanda.

There was a gate in the picket fence; I unlatched it and went along the path to the porch and rang the bell. The guy who opened the door was in his mid-to-late thirties, long and lean and intense-looking. He had a clump of dry black hair that drooped down on both sides of his narrow face like a bush that had died for lack of nourishment. His skin had a whitish pallor, there were the vestiges of pain in his eyes, and he carried a cane in his left hand—testimony to the truth of his statement that he'd been ill.

He said, "You're the detective?" and I said I was and he said, "I'm Michael Kiskadon, please come in."

I went in. A big family room opened off the entryway, across the rear of the house; Kiskadon led me in there, moving slowly with the aid of his cane, favoring his left leg. Windows with rattan blinds rolled up at their tops let you see Twin Peaks straight ahead and, off to the left, the ugly science-fictional skeleton of the Sutro telecommunications tower. Incoming sunlight made streaks and splashes across some nondescript furniture and a row of potted ferns and Wandering Jews set inside wicker stands.

"Some coffee?" Kiskadon asked. "My wife made a fresh pot before she went shopping."

"Thanks, but I've already had plenty."

He nodded. "Well—thank you for coming. As you can see, I'm not really fit for travel yet."

"Medical problems, you said?"

"Yes. I'm a diabetic—diabetes mellitus. Do you know what that is?"

"I've heard of it."

"Well, I have a severe form of the disease, a disorder of carbohydrate metabolism. Hyperglycemia, glycosuria—you name it, I had it or still have it. I was in the hospital for a month." He gave me a wry, mirthless smile. "I damn near died," he said.

What can you say to that? I said inadequately, "But it's under control now?"

"More or less, assuming there aren't any more complications." He sank down on the arm of an overstuffed Naugahyde couch. "Look, I'm not after sympathy or pity. My medical problems don't have anything to do with why I want a detective. Except that they helped me make up my mind to call you. I've been thinking about it for some time."

"I don't understand, Mr. Kiskadon."

"I almost died, as I said. I could still die before my time. There are some things I have to know before that happens, things that are important to me."

"Yes?"

"About my father. I never knew him, you see. He and my mother separated a month or so after I was conceived, and she moved back to Philadelphia, where her people were. She refused to tell my father she was pregnant."

"Why?"

"She was very bitter about the split; it was my father's idea to end their marriage, not hers. She had always wanted a child and he'd been against it. I was a planned accident on her part, I think." But he seemed not to have inherited any of his mother's bitterness toward his father; in his voice now was a kind of intense yearning; for what, I couldn't gauge yet.

I asked, "Did she tell him after you were born?"

"She never had the chance. She died giving birth to me."

"I see."

"I was raised by my mother's sister and her husband," Kiskadon said. "They legally adopted me, gave me their name. My aunt hated my father, even blamed him for my mother's death; she also vowed not to tell him about me. He died without ever knowing he had fathered a son."

"So it's not that you don't know who he was," I said. That was what I'd begun to think he was leading up to: a search for his roots, for the identity of his old man.

"No, it's not that at all. Uncle Ned told me the truth two years ago, after my aunt died. He said he didn't think it was right that I go through the rest of my life believing my natural father was killed in Korea, which was what I'd always been told."

"Did you make any effort to contact him, once you knew?"

The wry, mirthless smile again. "It was far too late by then," he said. "But a few months later I had a job offer in San Francisco and I accepted it. It took me a while after I was settled, but I managed to make contact with my father's widow, the woman he married after his divorce from my mother. I also located the man who'd been his attorney. Neither of them could or would tell me what I need to know."

"And that is?"

"Why he shot himself," Kiskadon said.

"Suicide?"

"Yes. With a handgun."

"Where was this?"

"At his home here in the city."

"How long ago?"

"In 1949, when I was four years old."

I stared at him. "Nineteen . . . did you say *forty-nine?*"

"That's right. December 10, 1949."

Well, Christ, I thought. I didn't say anything.

"I'm aware it might be impossible to find out the truth after thirty-five years," he said, "but I have to try. It's important to me—I told you that. It's . . . oh hell, I might as well

4

admit it: it's become an obsession. I *have* to know why he killed himself."

I still didn't say anything.

"I'll pay you well," he said. "I'm a design engineer for Bechtel; I make seventy-five thousand dollars a year when I'm working full-time."

"I'm not thinking about money, Mr. Kiskadon," I said. "The kind of job you want done . . . it's an exercise in futility and I'd be a liar if I told you otherwise. I can understand why you want to go ahead with it but I don't think I'm the right man to—"

"But you are the right man," he said. He stood up again and made an emphatic gesture with his cane. "You're *exactly* the right man."

"I don't understand."

"Come into my office. I want you to see something."

I shrugged and let him lead me into an adjacent room that had an L-shaped desk covered with computer equipment, a recliner chair, a table with a rack of pipes on it, and a big, glass-fronted bookcase along one wall. What was in the bookcase caught my eye immediately. I glanced at Kiskadon, and he said, "Go ahead, take a look," so I went over there and opened the glass doors and took a look.

Pulp magazines, upwards of two hundred of them. Mostly detective and mystery, with a sprinkling of adventure and Western titles. A pile of slick magazines, the top one a browning issue of *Collier's* from 1944. A shelf of books, hardcovers and paperbacks both, with the same author's name on the spines—a name I recognized. And a photograph in a silver frame, black and white and several years old, of a tall, angular man wearing horn-rimmed glasses and bearing a resemblance to Kiskadon, standing on somebody's lawn with a drink upraised in one hand. I turned to Kiskadon again.

"Yes," he said. "My father was Harmon Crane."

Harmon Crane. A name on the covers of scores of pulps in the thirties and forties; a name that sold magazines back then and was still selling them, to collectors such as myself.

5

One of the best writers of pulp fiction, whose blend of hard-boiled action and whacky humor had been rivaled only by Norbert Davis among the unsung heroes of the pulps. But Harmon Crane hadn't remained unsung because he hadn't remained a pulpster. He had graduated to such slicks as *Collier's, American Magazine,* and *The Saturday Evening Post;* and even more importantly, as far as aficionados of crime fiction were concerned, he had taken one of his pulp detectives, a screwball private eye named Johnny Axe, and fleshed him out and made him the hero of half a dozen novels that had sold remarkably well during the forties and that had been in print off and on ever since. Their titles, all of which were clever and outrageous puns, marched across the shelf behind me in their various editions: *Axe Marks the Spot, The Axe-Raye Murders, Axe for Trouble, Axe of Mercy, Don't Axe Me, Axe and Pains.*

I'd known that Crane had been a Bay Area resident since his college days at UC-Berkeley, and that he'd died here by his own hand around 1950; I had a vague memory of reading about his suicide in the papers back then, paying attention to it because of my interest in the pulps in general and his work in particular. But details about his personal life had been sketchy. I had always wondered what led such a successful writer to take his own life.

Crane was still one of my favorites; I read and collected his pulp work avidly. Which made things difficult as far as Michael Kiskadon was concerned. If his father had been anyone else I would have stuck to my guns and turned down his job offer. But because he had been sired by Harmon Crane, I could feel myself weakening. The prospect of poking around in Crane's life, even though he had been dead thirty-five years, held a perverse appeal. For some damn reason, the private lives of authors are endlessly fascinating to people like me who read their work.

Kiskadon was watching me in his intense way. "I started collecting his work as soon as I found out who he was," he said. "It took time and quite a lot of money, but I have just

about everything now; I'm only missing a dozen or so pulps. He wrote close to two hundred and fifty stories for the pulp market, you know."

I nodded. "Sold his first to *Black Mask* in 1933, while he was still at Berkeley."

"Yes. He was pre-med at the time." The intensity in Kiskadon's expression had been joined by eagerness: he was pretty sure he had me now. "I knew you'd remember him. A well-known detective who collects pulp magazines . . . well, now you see what I meant when I said you're exactly the right man for the job."

"Uh-huh."

"Will you take it, then?"

"I'm leaning that way." I glanced again at the photograph of Harmon Crane—the first I'd ever seen of him. He didn't look anything like the mental image I had formulated; he looked like a schoolteacher, or maybe an accountant. "Let's go sit down and talk. I've got a lot of questions."

We went back into the family room. Kiskadon sat on the couch and I sat in the closest chair, a creaky rocker that made me feel like an old fart in a retirement facility—the California Home for the Curmudgeonly, Kerry might have said. I watched Kiskadon light up a pipe. His tobacco smelled like chicken droppings; Eberhardt would have loved it.

I said, "First of all, what do you know about the suicide?"

"Very little. Just what my uncle told me, what I read in old newspapers at the library, and what I was able to find out from his lawyer. His widow wouldn't talk about it at all."

"He shot himself in his house, you said?"

"Yes. In his office."

"Where was he living at the time?"

"North Beach. Up near Coit Tower."

"Is the house still there?"

"No. There's an apartment building on the site now."

"What time of day did it happen?"

"Sometime around eight P.M."

7

"Was anybody else in the house at the time?"

"No. His wife was out to dinner with a friend."

"Just the two of them lived there?"

"Yes. My father had no other children."

"Who found his body?"

"His wife, her friend, and the lawyer."

"How did the lawyer happen to be there?"

"My father called him and asked him to come over. He arrived just as Mrs. Crane and the friend returned home."

"This friend—what's his name?"

"Adam Porter. He was Mrs. Crane's art teacher."

"Is he still alive?"

"No. He died in 1971."

"And the lawyer's name?"

"Thomas Yankowski."

Ah Christ, I thought, old Yank-'Em-Out.

Kiskadon said, "You look as if you know him."

"I know him, all right," I said. "We've had a few dealings in the past."

"You don't like him?"

"Not one bit."

"Neither did I. A sour old bastard."

"Yeah." Yank-'Em-Out Yankowski, the scourge of the legal profession and the bosom buddy of every slum landlord within a fifty-mile radius of San Francisco. He was retired now, but in his day he had specialized in landlord-tenant relationships, usually working for the landlords but occasionally playing the other side when there was enough money involved. He had boasted publicly that there wasn't a lease written he couldn't break, or a tenant he couldn't evict. The name Yank-'Em-Out had been tacked onto him as a pejorative, but he had taken a liking to it and used it as a kind of unofficial slogan. "How did he happen to be Harmon Crane's lawyer?"

"I don't know."

"Did he give you any hint what sort of legal service he might have been providing?"

"No."

"Did he say what Crane wanted to see him about the night of the suicide?"

"Only that my father seemed distraught, that he wanted someone to talk to."

"Were the two of them also friends?"

"That's what I gathered."

"But your father *didn't* wait to talk to Yankowski?"

"No. He . . . was drunk that night. Maybe that explains it."

"Maybe. Did he leave a note?"

"Yes. They found it in his typewriter when they broke in."

"Broke in?"

"The office door was locked from the inside," Kiskadon said. "His office was on the second floor, so they couldn't get in any other way."

"Were the windows locked too?"

"I don't know. Does it matter?"

"I suppose not. What did the suicide note say?"

"Nothing specific. Just that he felt he'd be better off dead. It was only a few lines long."

"He'd been despondent, then?"

"For several weeks. He'd been drinking heavily."

"Any clues as to why?"

"According to Yankowski, my father wouldn't discuss it with anyone. Yankowski thinks it was some sort of writer's block; my father wrote almost nothing during the last six weeks of his life. But I find that theory difficult to believe, considering how much fiction he produced. And how much writing meant to him—others have told me that." Kiskadon's pipe had gone out; he paused to relight it. "In any case, his motive had to have been personal."

"Why do you say that?"

"Well, I don't see how it could have been financial. He had contracts for two new Johnny Axe novels, and there was a film deal in the works. There was also talk of doing a Johnny Axe radio show."

"Uh-huh. Well, if anyone knows the reason, it's his widow. Maybe I can pry it out of her. Where does she live?"

"In Berkeley. With her niece, a woman named Marilyn Dubek." He gave me the address from memory and I wrote it down in my notebook.

"Is her name still Crane?"

"Yes. Amanda Crane. She never remarried."

"Was your father her first husband?"

"Yes."

"How long were they married?"

"Two years. The split with my mother wasn't over her, if that's what you're thinking. They didn't even know each other at the time of the separation."

"What did cause the split with your mother?"

"She had extravagant ways; that was the main reason. She was a social animal—parties, nightclubs, that sort of thing—and my father liked his privacy. They just weren't very well matched, I guess."

"How long were *they* married?"

"Four years."

"Your father's first marriage?"

"No. His second."

"Who was his first wife?"

"A woman named Ellen Corneal. He married her while they were both in college. It didn't last very long."

"Why not?"

"I'm not sure. Incompatibility again, I think."

"Do you know what happened to her?"

"No."

"Back to Yankowski. Where did you talk to him?"

"At his home. He lives in St. Francis Wood."

"How willing was he to see you?"

"Willing enough," Kiskadon said. "I called and explained who I was, and he invited me over. He was a little standoffish in person, but he answered all my questions."

"Can you give me the names of any of your father's friends in 1949?"

"He apparently didn't have any close friends."

"What about other writers?"

"Well, he wasn't a joiner but he did know some of the other writers in the Bay Area. I managed to track down a couple who knew him casually, but they weren't any help. They only saw him at an occasional literary function."

"You might as well give me their names anyway."

He did and I wrote them down. One was familiar; the other wasn't. Neither had written for the pulps, unless the unfamiliar guy had cranked out stories under a pseudonym. I asked Kiskadon about that, and he said no, the man had written confession stories and fact articles for more than thirty years and was now retired and living on Social Security.

Be a writer, I thought, make big money and secure your future.

I spent the next five minutes settling with Kiskadon on my fee and the size of my retainer, and filling out the standard contract form I'd brought with me. He signed the form, and was working on a check when I heard the sound of a key in the front door lock. A moment later a woman came inside.

She stopped when she saw me and said, "Oh," but not as if she were startled. She was a few years younger than Kiskadon, brown-haired, on the slender side except for flaring hips encased in a pair of too-tight jeans. Why women with big bottoms persist in wearing tight pants is a riddle of human nature the Sphinx couldn't answer, so I didn't even bother to try. Otherwise she was pretty enough in a Bonnie Bedelia sort of way.

Kiskadon said, "Lynn, hi. This is the detective I told you about." He gave her my name, which impressed her about as much as if he'd given her a carpet tack. "He's going to take on the job."

She gave me a doubtful look. Then she said, "Good. That's fine, dear," in that tone of voice wives use when they're humoring their spouses.

"He'll get to the truth if anyone can," Kiskadon said.

She didn't answer that; instead she looked up at me again. "How much are you charging?"

Practical lady. I told her, and she thought about it, biting her lip, and seemed to decide that I wasn't being *too* greedy. She nodded and said to him, "I'll get the groceries out of the car. We'll have lunch pretty soon."

"Good, I'm starved."

She asked me, "Will you be joining us?"

"Thanks, but I'd better get to work."

"You're perfectly welcome to stay. . . ."

"No. Thanks, anyway."

"Well," she said, and shrugged, and turned and went out with her rear end wiggling and waggling. You could almost hear the stretched threads creaking in the seams of her jeans.

Kiskadon gave me his check and his hand and an eager smile; he looked better than he had when I'd arrived—color in his cheeks, a kind of zest in his movements, as if my agreeing to investigate for him had worked like a rejuvenating medicine. I thought: That's me, the Good Samaritan. But I had taken the job as much for me as for him: so much for virtue and the milk of human kindness.

When I got outside, Mrs. Kiskadon was hefting an armload of Safeway sacks out of the trunk of a newish green Ford Escort parked in the driveway. She seemed to want to say something to me as I passed by, but whatever she saw when she glanced toward the porch changed her mind for her. All I got was a sober nod, which I returned in kind. I looked back at the porch myself as I opened the gate; she was on her way there carrying the grocery sacks, and Kiskadon was standing out in plain sight, leaning on his cane and looking past her at me, still smiling.

He waved as I went through the gate, but I didn't wave back. I'm not sure why.

TWO

St. Francis Wood was only a ten-minute drive, so I went there to see Yank-'Em-Out Yankowski first. Unlike Golden Gate Heights, the Wood is one of the city's ritzy neighborhoods, spread out along the lower, westward slope of Mt. Davidson and full of old money and the old codgers who'd accumulated it. Some of the houses in there had fine views of the ocean a couple of miles distant, but Yankowski's wasn't one of them. It was a Spanish-style job built down off San Juanito Way, bordered on one side by a high cypress hedge and on the other by a woody lot overgrown with eucalyptus trees; half-hidden by flowering bushes, more cypress, and a tangle of other vegetation. Either Yankowski was a bucolic at heart, which I doubted, or he liked plenty of privacy.

I parked at the curb in front and went down a set of curving stone stairs and onto a tile-floored porch. The front door looked like the one that barred the entrance to the castle in every B-grade horror film ever made: aged black wood, ironbound, with nail studs and an ornate latch. There wasn't any bell; I lifted a huge black-iron knocker and let it make a bang like a gun going off.

Immediately a dog began barking inside. It was a big dog, and it sounded mad as hell at having been disturbed. But it didn't bark for long; when the noise stopped I heard it moving, heard the click and scrape of its nails on stone or tile, and then it slammed into the door snarling and growling and burbling like Lewis Carroll's jabberwock. It probably had eyes of flame, too, and its drooling jaws would no doubt have enjoyed making a snicker-snack of my throat. If I'd been a burglar I would have run like hell. As it was I backed off a couple of paces. I am not crazy about dogs, especially vicious dogs like whatever monstrosity Yankowski kept in there.

It went right on snarling and burbling. Nobody came and

told it to shut up; nobody opened the door, either, for which I was properly grateful. I debated leaving one of my business cards, and decided against it; when I saw Yank-'Em-Out I wanted to catch him unprepared, just in case he *hadn't* told Michael Kiskadon everything he knew about Harmon Crane's suicide.

The thing in the house lunged against the door again, making it quiver and creak in protest. I said, "Stupid goddamn beast," but I said it under my breath while I was going back up the stairs.

Berkeley used to be a quiet, sleepy little college town, with tree-shaded side streets and big old houses as its main non-academic attraction. But its image had changed in the sixties, as a result of the flower children and radical politics fomented by the senseless war in Vietnam. In the seventies, Patty Hearst and the Symbionese Liberation Army had added a bizarre new dimension, which the media and the right-wingers had mushroomed into a silly reputation for Berkeley as the home of every left-wing nut group in the country. And in the eighties, it seemed to have become a magnet for a variety of criminals and the lunatic fringe: drug dealers, muggers, purse snatchers, burglars, pimps, panhandlers, bag ladies, bag men, flashers, acidheads, religious cultists, and just plain weirdos. Nowadays it had one of the highest crime rates in the Bay Area. And the downtown area centering on Telegraph Avenue near the university was a free daily freakshow. You could get high on marijuana just walking the sidewalks; and you were liable to see just about anything on a given day. The last time I'd been there I had seen, within the space of a single block, a filth-encrusted kid with bombed-out eyes reciting passages from the *Rubaiyat;* a guy dressed up like an Oriental potentate sitting cross-legged on the sidewalk with a myna bird perched on his shoulder, plucking out Willie Nelson tunes on a sitar; and a jolly old fellow in a yarmulke selling half a kilo of grass to an aging hippie couple, the female member of which was carrying an infant in a shoulder sling.

14

No more sleepy little college town: Berkeley had graduated to the big time. Welcome to urban America, babycakes.

Still, the old, saner Berkeley continued to exist in pockets up in the hills and down on the flats. The Cal campus was pretty much the same as it had always been, and the kids who went there were mostly good kids with their priorities on straight. Most of the residents were good people too, no matter what their politics happened to be. And the tree-shaded side streets and big old houses were still there, with the only difference being that now the houses had alarm systems, bars on their windows, triple locks on their doors, and maybe a handgun or a shotgun strategically placed inside. Driving along one of those old-Berkeley streets, you could almost believe things were as simple and uncomplicated as they had been in the days when this was just another college town. Almost.

The street Amanda Crane lived on was like that: it seemed a long, long way from the Telegraph Avenue freakshow, even though only a couple of miles separated them. It was off Ashby Avenue up near the fashionable Claremont Hotel: Linden Street, named after the ferny trees that lined it and that, here and there along its length, joined overhead to create a tunnel effect. The number Michael Kiskadon had given me was down toward the far end—a brown-shingled place at least half a century old, with a brick-and-dark-wood porch that had splashes of red bouganvillea growing over it. A massive willow and a couple of kumquat trees grew in the front yard, providing plenty of shade.

A woman was sitting on an old-fashioned swing on the porch. But it wasn't until I parked the car and started along the walk that I had a good look at her: silver-haired, elderly, holding a magazine in her lap so that it was illuminated by dappled sunlight filtering down through the leaves of the willow tree.

She lifted her head and smiled at me as I came up onto the porch. I returned the smile, moving over to stand near her with my back to the porch railing. Inside the house, a vacuum

cleaner was making a high-pitched screeching noise that would probably have done things to my nerves if I had been any closer to it.

The woman on the swing was in her mid-sixties, small, delicate, with pale and finely wrinkled skin that made you think of a fragile piece of bone china that had been webbed with tiny cracks. She had never been beautiful, but I thought that once, thirty-five years ago, she would have been quite striking. She was still striking, but in a different sort of way. There was a certain serenity in her expression and in her faded blue eyes, the kind of look you sometimes see on the faces of the ultra-devout—the look of complete inner peace. She was wearing an old-fashioned blue summer dress buttoned to the throat. A pair of rimless spectacles were tilted forward on a tiny nose dusted with powder to dull if not hide its freckles.

"Hello," she said, smiling.

"Hello. Mrs. Crane—Amanda Crane?"

"Why, yes. Do I know you?"

"No, ma'am."

"You're not a salesman, are you? This is my niece's house and she can't abide salesmen."

"No, I'm not a salesman. I'm here to see you."

"Really? About what?"

"Harmon Crane."

"Oh," she said in a pleased way. "You're a fan, then."

"Fan?"

"Of Harmon's writing. His fans come to see me once in a while; one of them even wrote an article about me for some little magazine. You *are* one of his fans, aren't you?"

"Yes, I am," I said truthfully. "Your husband was a very good writer."

"Oh yes, so everyone says."

"Don't you think so?"

"Well," she said, and shrugged delicately, and closed her magazine—*Ladies' Home Journal*—and took off her glasses. "Harmon had rather a risqué sense of humor, you know."

"Yes, I know."

"Yes," she said.

"You *did* read his fiction, though?"

"Some of it. His magazine stories . . . some of those were nice. There was one about a young couple on vacation in Yosemite, I think it was in *The Saturday Evening Post.* Do you remember that story?"

"No, I'm afraid I don't."

"It was very funny. Not at all risqué. I can't seem to remember the title."

"Was your husband funny in person too?"

"Funny? Oh yes, he liked to make people laugh."

"Would you say he was basically a happy man?"

"Yes, I would."

"And you and he were happy together?"

"Quite happy. We had a lovely marriage. He was devoted to me, you know. And I to him."

"No problems of any kind between you?"

"Oh no. No."

"But he did have other problems," I said gently. "Would you know what they were?"

"Problems?" she said.

"That led him to take his own life."

She sat motionless, still smiling slightly; she might not have heard me. "I think it was 'Never Argue with a Woman,'" she said at length.

"Pardon?"

"The story of Harmon's that I liked in *The Saturday Evening Post.* Yes, it must have been 'Never Argue with a Woman.'"

"Mrs. Crane, do you know why your husband shot himself?"

Silence. A little brown-and-yellow bird swooped down out of one of the kumquat trees and landed on the porch railing; she watched as it hopped along, chittering softly to itself, its head darting from side to side. Her hands, folded together just under her breasts, had a poised, suspended look.

17

"Mrs. Crane?"

I moved when I spoke, startling the bird; it went away. The last of her smile went away with it. She blinked, and her hands settled on top of the copy of *Ladies' Home Journal*. Unconsciously she began to twist the small diamond ring on the third finger of her left hand.

"No," she said. "No."

"You don't know why?"

"I won't talk about that. Not about that."

"It's important, Mrs. Crane. If you could just give me some idea. . . ."

"No," she said. Then she said, "Oh, wait, I was wrong. It *wasn't* 'Never Argue with a Woman' that I liked so much. Of course it wasn't. It was 'The Almost Perfect Vacation.' How silly of me to have got the two mixed up."

She smiled at me again, but it was a different kind of smile this time; her eyes seemed to be saying, "Please don't talk about this anymore, please don't hurt me." I felt her pain—that had always been one of my problems, too much empathy—and it made me feel like one of the sleazy types that prowled Telegraph Avenue.

But I didn't quit probing at her, not just yet. I might not like myself sometimes, but that had never stopped me from doing my job. If it had I would have gone out of business years ago.

I said, "I'm sorry, Mrs. Crane. I won't bring that up again. Is it all right if I ask you some different questions?"

"Well . . ."

"Do you still see any old friends of your husband's?"

She bit her lip. "We didn't have many friends," she said. "We had each other, but . . . it wasn't . . ." The words trailed off into silence.

"There's no one you're still in touch with?"

"Only Stephen. He still comes to see me sometimes."

"Stephen?"

"Stephen Porter."

"Would he be any relation to Adam Porter?"

18

"Why, yes—Adam's brother. Did you know Adam?"

"No, ma'am. He was mentioned to me as a friend of your husband's."

"More my friend than Harmon's, I must say."

"Adam, you mean?"

"Yes. He was my art teacher. He was a painter, you know."

"No, I didn't know."

"A very good painter. Oils. I was much better with watercolors. Still life, mostly. Fruit and such."

"Do you still paint?"

"Oh no, not in years and years."

"Is Stephen Porter also a painter?"

"No, he's a sculptor. He teaches, too; it's very difficult for sculptors to make a living these days unless they also teach. I imagine that's the case with most artists, don't you?"

"Yes, ma'am. Does he have a studio?"

"Oh, of course."

"In what city?"

"In San Francisco."

"Could you tell me the address?"

"Are you going to see Stephen?"

"I'd like to, yes."

"Well, you tell him it's been quite a while since he came to visit. Months, now. Will you tell him that?"

"I will."

"North Beach," she said.

"Ma'am?"

"Stephen's studio. It's in North Beach." She smiled reminiscently. "Harmon and I used to live in North Beach—a lovely old house near Coit Tower, with trees all around. He so loved his privacy."

"Yes, ma'am."

"It's gone now. Torn down long ago."

"Can you tell me the address of Stephen's studio?"

"I don't believe I remember it," she said. "But I'm sure it's in the telephone directory."

Inside the house, the vacuum cleaner stopped its screeching; there was a hushed quality to the silence that followed. I broke it by saying, "I understand Thomas Yankowski was also a friend of your husband's."

"Well, he was Harmon's attorney."

"Did your husband have any special reason to need a lawyer?"

"Well, a woman tried to sue him once, for plagiarism. It was a silly thing, one of those . . . what do you call them?"

"Nuisance suits?"

"Yes. A nuisance suit. He met Thomas somewhere, while he was doing legal research for one of his books, I think it was, and Thomas handled the matter for him."

"Were they also friends?"

"I suppose they were. Although we seldom saw Thomas socially."

"Does he ever come to visit you now?"

"Thomas? No, not since I refused him."

"How do you mean, 'refused him?'"

"When he asked me to marry him."

"When was this?"

"Not long after . . . well, a long time ago."

"And you turned him down?"

"Oh yes," she said. "Harmon was the only man I ever loved. I've never remarried; I never could."

"You and Mr. Crane had no children, is that right?"

She said demurely, "We weren't blessed that way, no."

"But your husband did have a son by a previous marriage."

"Michael," she said, and nodded. "I was quite surprised when he came to see me. I never knew Harmon had a son. Michael never knew it either. Michael . . . I can't seem to recall his last name . . ."

"Kiskadon."

"Yes. An odd name. I wish he'd come back for another visit; he was only here that one time. Such a nice boy. Harmon would have been proud of him, I'm sure."

"Did you know Michael's mother?"

"No. Harmon was already divorced from her when I met him."

"Did you know his first wife?"

"First wife?"

"Ellen Corneal."

"No, you're mistaken," she said. "Harmon was never married to a woman named Ellen."

"But he was. While they were attending UC . . ."

"No," she said positively. "He was only married once before we took our vows. To Michael's mother, Susan. Only once."

"Is that what he told you?"

She didn't have the chance to answer my question. The front door opened just then and a woman came out—a dumpy woman in her forties, with dyed black hair bound up with a bandanna and a face like Petunia Pig. She said, "I thought I heard voices out here," and gave me a suspicious look. "Who are you? What are you doing here?"

"We've been talking about Harmon," Mrs. Crane said.

"Yes," I said, "we have," and let it go at that.

"God, another one of *those*," the dumpy woman said. "You haven't been upsetting her, have you? You fan types always upset her."

"I don't think so, no."

She turned to Mrs. Crane. "Auntie? *Has* he been upsetting you?"

"No, Marilyn. Do I look upset, dear?"

"Well, I think you'd better come inside now."

"I don't want to come inside, dear."

"We'll have some tea. Earl Grey's."

"Well, tea *would* be nice. Perhaps the gentleman . . ."

"The gentleman can come back some other time," Petunia Pig said. She was looking at me as she spoke and her expression said: I'm lying for her benefit. Go away and don't come back.

"But he might want to ask me some more questions. . . ."

21

"No more questions. Not today."

Mrs. Crane smiled up at me. "It has been very nice talking to you," she said.

"Same here. I appreciate your time, Mrs. Crane."

"Not at all. I enjoy talking about Harmon."

"Of course you do, Auntie," Petunia Pig said, "but you know it isn't good for you when it goes on too long. Come along, now. Upsy-daisy."

She helped Mrs. Crane up off the swing, putting an arm protectively around her shoulders, and Mrs. Crane smiled at her and then smiled at me and said, "Marilyn takes such good care of me," and all of a sudden I realized, with a profound sense of shock, that her air of serenity did not come from inner peace at all; it and her smile both were the product of a mental illness.

The niece, Marilyn, glared at me over her shoulder as she walked Mrs. Crane to the door. I moved quickly to the stairs, went down them, and when I looked back they were gone inside. The door banged shut behind them.

I sat in the car for a couple of minutes, a little shaken, staring up at the house and remembering Mrs. Crane's smile and the pain that had come into her eyes when I pressed her about her husband's suicide. That must have been what did it to her, what unsettled her mind and made her unable to care for herself. And that meant she had been like this for thirty-five years. Thirty-five *years!*

I felt like a horse's ass.

No. I felt like its droppings.

THREE

As I drove away from there, back down Ashby, I cursed Michael Kiskadon. Why the hell hadn't he told me

about his stepmother's condition? But the anger didn't last long. Pretty soon I thought: Quit jumping to conclusions; maybe *he* never realized it at all. She looked and sounded normal enough; it was only when you analyzed what she said and the way she said it that you understood how off-key it was. Look how long it had taken me to realize the truth, and at that I might not have tumbled if it hadn't been for the way the niece treated her.

Some detective I was. There were times when I couldn't detect a fart in a Skid Row beanery.

It was almost one-thirty when I came back across the Bay Bridge into San Francisco. I took the Broadway exit that leads to North Beach, stopped at the first service station off the freeway, and looked up Stephen Porter in the public telephone directory. Only one listed—and just the number, no street address. I fished up a dime and dialed the number. Nobody answered.

Yeah, I thought, *that* figures.

The prospect of food had no appeal, but my stomach was rumbling and it seemed a wise idea to fill the empty spaces; I hadn't had anything to eat all day except for an orange with my breakfast coffee at eight A.M. I drove on through the Broadway tunnel and stopped at a place on Polk, where I managed to swallow a tuna-fish-on-rye and a glass of iced tea. I wanted a beer instead of the iced tea, but I was on short rations again where the suds were concerned; after losing a lot of weight earlier in the year I had started to pork up a little again, and I was damned if I was going to get reacquainted with my old nemisis, the beer belly. So it was one bottle of Lite per day now—and the way this day was progressing, I was going to need my one bottle even more later than I did now.

From the restaurant I went down to Civic Center, wasted fifteen minutes looking for a place to park, and finally got into the microfilm room at the main library. Kiskadon had told me the date of his father's death was December 10, 1949. San Francisco had had four newspapers back then—*News, Call-*

Bulletin, Chronicle, and *Examiner;* I requested the issues of December 11 and 12, 1949, from all four. Then I sat down at one of the magnifying machines and proceeded to abuse my eyes and give myself a headache squinting at page after page of blurry newsprint.

The facts of Harmon Crane's suicide—or at least the facts that had been made public—were pretty much as Kiskadon had given them to me. On the night of December 10, Amanda Crane had gone out to dinner on Fisherman's Wharf with Adam Porter; Harmon Crane had been invited but had declined to accompany them. According to Porter, Crane had seemed withdrawn and depressed and had been drinking steadily all day. "I had no inkling that he might be contemplating suicide," Porter was quoted as saying. "Harmon just never struck me as the suicidal type."

Porter and Mrs. Crane had returned to the secluded North Beach house at 8:45. Thomas Yankowski arrived just after they entered the premises; he had been summoned by a call from Crane, who had "sounded desperate and not altogether coherent," and had rushed right over. Alarmed by this, Mrs. Crane began calling her husband's name. When he didn't respond, Yankowski and Porter ran upstairs, where they found the door to Crane's office locked from the inside. Their concern was great enough by this time to warrant breaking in. And inside they had found Crane slumped over his desk, dead of a gunshot wound to the right temple.

The weapon, a .22 caliber Browning target automatic, was clenched in his hand. It was his gun, legally registered to him; he had been fond of target shooting and owned three such small-caliber firearms. A typed note "spattered with the writer's blood," according to some yellow journalist on the *Call,* lay on top of Crane's typewriter. It said: "I can't go on any longer. Can't sleep, can't eat, can't work. I think I'm losing my mind. Life terrifies me more than death. I will be better off dead and Mandy will be better off without me."

There were no quotes from Amanda Crane in any of the news stories; she was said to be in seclusion, under a doctor's

care—which usually indicated severe trauma. Yankowski and Porter both expressed shock and dismay at the suicide. Porter said, "Harmon hadn't been himself lately—withdrawn and drinking too much. We thought it was some sort of a slump, perhaps writer's block. We never believed it would come to this." Yankowski said, "The only explanation I can find is that he ran out of words. Writing meant more to Harmon than anything else in this world. Not being able to write would be a living death to a man of his temperament."

No one else who knew Crane had any better guesses to make. He had been closemouthed about whatever was troubling him, and evidently confided in no one at all. As far as anyone knew, his reasons for embracing death had died with him.

So how was *I* supposed to find out what they were, thirty-five years later? What did it matter, really, why he had knocked himself off? We all die sooner or later, some with cause, some without. Ashes to ashes, dust to dust, and who the hell cares in the long run?

Amanda Crane cared. Michael Kiskadon cared. And maybe I cared too, a little: there's always some damn fool like me to care about things that don't matter in the long run.

I left the library, picked up my car and the overtime parking ticket flapping under the windshield wiper, said a few words out loud about the way the city of San Francisco treats its citizens, and drove back up Van Ness to O'Farrell Street. The office I share with Eberhardt is on O'Farrell, not far from Van Ness, and in the next block is a parking garage that by comparison with the garages farther downtown offers a dirt-cheap monthly rate. I put the car in my alloted space on the ground floor and walked back to my building.

The place doesn't look like much from the outside: bland and respectable in a shabby sort of way. It doesn't look like much on the inside either. The ground floor belongs to a real estate company, the second floor belongs to an outfit that makes custom shirts ("The Slim-Taper Look is the Right Look"), and the third and top floor belongs to Eberhardt and

me. That floor is a converted loft that once housed an art school, which is why it has a skylight in the ceiling. Very classy, an office with a skylight—except when it rains. Then the noise the rain makes beating down on the glass is so loud you have to yell when you're talking on the telephone.

Eberhardt was talking on the telephone when I came in—settled back in his chair with his feet up on his desk—but he wasn't yelling; he was crooning and cooing into the receiver like a constipated dove. Which meant that he was talking to Wanda. He always crooned and cooed when he talked to Wanda—a man fifty-five years old, divorced, a tough ex-cop. It was pretty disgusting to see and hear.

But he was in love, or thought he was. Wanda Jaworski, an employee of the downtown branch of Macy's—the footwear department. They had met in a supermarket a couple of months ago, when he dropped a package of chicken parts on her foot. This highly romantic beginning had evolved into a whirlwind courtship and a (probably drunken) proposal of marriage. They hadn't set a definite date yet; Wanda was still assembling her trousseau. Or "truss-o," as she put it, which sounded like some kind of device for people with hernias. Wanda was not long on brains. Nor was Wanda long on sophistication; Wanda, in fact, was coarse, silly, and an incessant babbler. Nor was she long on looks, unless you happen to covet overweight forty-five-year-old women with double chins and big behinds and the kind of bright yellow hair that looks as if it belongs on a Raggedy Ann doll. What Wanda *was* long on was chest. She had the biggest chest I have ever seen, a chest that would have dwarfed Mamie Van Doren's, a chest that would have shamed Dolly Parton's, a chest among chests.

It was Kerry's considered opinion that Eberhardt was not in love with Wanda so much as he was in love with Wanda's chest. He was fascinated by it—or them. Whenever he and Wanda were together he seemed unable to take his eyes off it—or them. It was also Kerry's considered opinion that if he married her, he would be making a monumental mistake.

"What he's doing," she'd said to me in her typically caustic way on the occasion of our first meeting Wanda, "is making a molehill out of a couple of mountains."

I tended to agree, but there wasn't much I could do about it. You don't tell your business partner, your best friend for more than thirty years, that he is contemplating marriage to a pea-brained twit. You don't tell him that he can't see the forest for the chest. You don't tell him anything; you just keep your mouth shut and hope that he comes to his senses before it's too late.

He waggled a hand at me as I crossed to my desk. I didn't feel like doing any waggling in return, so I nodded at him and then made a slight detour when I saw that he had a pot of coffee on the hot plate. I poured myself a cup and sat down with it and tried calling Stephen Porter's number again. Still no answer. So then I just sat there, sipping coffee and waiting for Eberhardt to come back to the real world.

The office was big, about twenty feet square; otherwise it wasn't anything to get excited about. The walls and the carpet we'd put down ourselves were a funny beige color that clashed with some hideous mustard yellow fiberboard file cabinets Eberhardt had bought on a whim and refused to repaint. The furnishings consisted of our two desks, some chairs, my file cabinets and his, and an old-fashioned water cooler with a bottle of Alhambra on it that we used to make the coffee. And suspended from the middle of the ceiling was a light fixture that resembled nothing so much as a bunch of brass testicles soldered onto a grappling hook, which someday I was going to tear down and hurl out a window. Not the window behind Eberhardt's desk, which looked out on the blank brick wall of the building next door; the one behind my desk, which had a splendid view of the backside of the Federal Building down on Golden Gate Avenue, not to metion the green copper dome of City Hall further downhill at Civic Center.

Spade and Archer, I thought, circa 1929. Only there was no black bird and no Joel Cairo or Caspar Gutman or Brigid O'Shaughnessy in *our* lives. There was only Wanda the Foot-

wear Queen, and some poor bastard of a writer who had gotten into the Christmas spirit one December night three and a half decades ago by putting a bullet through his brain.

Eberhardt muttered something into the telephone receiver, cupped his hand over it, and poked his jowly, graying head in my direction. "Hey, paisan," he said, "you got anything on for tomorrow night?"

"I don't know, I don't think so. Why?"

"How about the four of us going out to dinner? Wanda knows this great little out-of-the-way place."

I hesitated. The last thing I wanted to do tomorrow night was to have dinner with Wanda. The last thing Kerry would want to do *ever* was to have dinner with Wanda; Kerry disliked the Footwear Queen even more than I did, and was not always careful to hide her feelings. The four of us had had dinner together once, not long after Eberhardt had found true love via a package of Foster Farms drumsticks, and it had not been a memorable evening. "The only thing bigger than that woman's tits," Kerry had said later, "is her mouth. I wonder if she talks the whole time they're in bed together too?" Which was something I still didn't want to think about.

I said lamely, "Uh, well, I don't know, Eb . . ."

"Kerry's free, isn't she?"

"Well, I'm not sure . . ."

"You said last Friday she'd be free all this week. How about it, paisan? We'll make a night of it."

A night of it, I thought. I said No, no, *no!* inside my head, but my mouth said, "Sure, okay, if Kerry's not doing anything." It was a mistake; I knew it was a mistake and that I would pay for it when I told Kerry, but I hadn't wanted to offend him. He got grumpy when he was offended and there was something I needed him to do for me.

He said, "All set, then," and did a little more crooning and cooing to Wanda. I half expected him to play kissy-face with her when the coversation finally ended, a spectacle that would have made me throw up, but it didn't happen. I think

he said, "Bye-bye, sugar," which was bad enough. Then he took his feet down and gave me a sappy, lovestruck grin.

"That was Wanda," he said.

"Yeah," I said.

"What a peach," he said.

What a pair, I thought. Wanda's chest and him. I asked him, "Anything happen today?"

"Nah, it's been quiet. Some woman called for you; wouldn't leave her name, wouldn't say what she wanted. Said it was a private matter and she'd call back."

"Uh-huh."

"Only other call was from that asshole runs the credit company out in Daly City."

"Dennison? What did he want?"

"Another repo job. A new Jaguar, can you believe it?"

"I can believe it. You take the job?"

"Sure I took it."

"That's good."

"I never drove a Jag before," he said. "That's the only reason." He shook his head. "Repossesing cars. For Christ's sake, what kind of job is that for a detective?"

"The bread-and-butter kind."

"Nickels and dimes, you mean. Hell, I don't want Wanda to have to work after we're married. I want to buy her the kind of things she deserves."

Like a tent for her chest and a sack for her face, I thought, and immediately felt guilty. He was in love with her, after all. Maybe she had her good points. Maybe underneath all that chest there beat a heart of pure gold.

Maybe the Pope is Jewish, I thought.

Eberhardt said, "So how'd it go with you? The guy up on Twelfth Avenue?"

"I took him on," I said, and explained what kind of job it was and what I'd been doing all day.

"A nut case," he said, grimacing. "You better make sure his check doesn't bounce before you do any more work."

"It won't bounce."

"It's the pulp angle, right? That's why you took it on."

"In the beginning. Now it's more than that."

"It always is with you." Another headshake. "Nut cases and car repos—what a hell of a glamorous business we got going for us here."

"You want glamour? Go to work for the Pinkertons."

"Yeah, sure, and wind up a security guard in a bank."

"Then don't bitch."

He sighed, rummaged around among the clutter on his desk, found one of his pipes, took it apart, and ran a pipe cleaner through the stem. "Old Yank-'Em-Out Yankowski," he said musingly. "What a miserable son of a bitch *he* was, in and out of court."

"He probably still is."

"You ever have dealings with him?"

"Some."

"Me too. A goddamn bloodsucker. You know, I thought he was dead. Didn't he have a heart attack or something a couple of years ago?"

"I don't know, did he?"

"Seems I heard he did. Too bad he survived."

"Bad karma, Eb."

"Huh?"

"Never mind. Listen, how far back do the Department's files go? Would they still have the inspector's report on a routine suicide in 1949?"

"Probably. Never get rid of anything—that was the policy before I retired." Eb had taken an early retirement from the cops less than a year ago—he was a year older than me, fifty-five—and he'd been my partner for about six months. He still had plenty of friends in the Department, plenty of old favors to call in; there wasn't much going on at the Hall of Justice that he didn't know about and nothing much in the way of official documentation that he couldn't lay hands on. "I suppose you want a look at the Crane report."

"Right."

"Why bother? It won't tell you any more than the news-paper stories."

"It might. Could be something in it, some hint of Crane's motive, that the reporters didn't get."

He shrugged. "Okay, I'll get it for you—if it hasn't been lost, stolen, or misfiled. Thirty-five years is a long time."

"Don't I know it. How soon?"

"Tomorrow sometime."

I nodded. My watch said it was almost four-thirty; I finished my coffee and lifted myself out of the chair. "I'd better get moving. You mind hanging around until five and locking up?"

"No problem. Where you off to?"

"A talk with Yank-'Em-Out, if he's home by now. And then dinner with Kerry."

"Dinner, yeah," he said. "Don't forget tomorrow night."

"I won't forget," I said. "Kerry won't let me."

And that was the truth in more ways than one.

FOUR

This time when I rang the bell at the Yankowski house, there was somebody home besides the fire-breathing jab-berwock. The thing started up in there again, whiffling and burbling, but the noise came distantly, from the back of the place, and never got any closer. Pretty soon the door opened on a chain and a white female face topped by frizzy gray hair appeared in the opening. It said suspiciously, "Yes? What is it?"

"I'd like to see Mr. Yankowski."

"Is he expecting you?"

"No, but I think he'll see me. Just tell him it concerns Harmon Crane and his son."

"Your name?"

I held up one of my business cards. A chubby white arm slithered out through the door opening, snatched the card, and then disappeared with it. The face said, "Wait, please," after which it, too, disappeared and the door snicked shut.

I stood there. A thin breeze off the ocean carried the smells of eucalyptus and jasmine; it was that kind of early evening. Inside the house, the jabberwock continued to make a lot of distant noise, including a couple of thumps and a faint hollow crash. Probably eating some furniture, I thought. Or maybe eating the housekeeper, if that was who owned the white face and the white arm and the frizzy gray hair; as far as I knew, Yankowski had never been married.

But no, the door opened again finally, still on its chain, and there she was. She said, "He'll see you. You can go on around back."

"Around back?"

"He's in the garden."

There were some stepping stones that led away from the tile porch, through jasmine shrubs and dwarf cypress pruned into eccentric shapes. All the windows of the house had iron bars bolted across them, I noticed: an added precaution to ease the usual city dweller's paranoia. In Yankowski's case, though, there was probably more to it than that. There must have been a couple of thousand people in the Bay Area with just cause to break into his house and murder him in his bed.

At the rear I found a high fence with a gate in it. From the top of the fence, another six feet or so of clear molded plastic curved up and then back to the house wall; the effect was of a kind of bubble that would enclose and also secure the garden within. I tried the gate latch, found it unlocked, and walked in.

The garden contained a twenty-foot square of well-barbered lawn, bordered on three sides by rose bushes and on the fourth by the rear staircase and a path leading from it to the gate. On the lawn were a Weber barbecue and some pieces of redwood outdoor furniture. And on one of the

chairs was old Yank-'Em-Out himself, sitting comfortably with his legs crossed, a drink in one hand and a fat green cigar in the other.

"Flip the lock on the gate when you close it," he said. "I unlocked it for you."

Yeah, I thought, paranoia. I shut the gate, flipped the lock, and went to where he was sitting. The rear of the house faced west and the sun was starting to set now over the Pacific; the glare of it coming through that plastic bubble overhead gave the enclosure an odd reddish tinge, as if it were artificially lighted. The glow made Yankowski look gnomish and feral, like a retired troll who had moved out from under his bridge to a house in the city. Which was a fanciful thought, but one that pleased me just the same.

My business card lay all by itself on a redwood table next to him; he tapped it with a crooked forefinger, not quite hard enough to knock the long gray ash off his cigar. "I'm honored," he said. "It isn't every day a famous private eye comes calling on me."

There was no irony or sarcasm in his voice. I didn't let any come into mine, either, when I said, "It isn't every day that I get to pay a call on a distinguished member of the legal profession."

"An honor for both of us, then. But we've met before, haven't we? I seem to recall that you worked for me once a few years ago."

"Just once. After that I worked for your opponents."

He thought that was funny; he had a fine sense of humor, Yank-'Em-Out did. He also had his own teeth, the bastard, and a fine head of dark brown hair with only a little gray at the temples—Grecian Formula, I thought; has to be—and a strong, lean body and not many more wrinkles than I've got. He had to be at least seventy, but he looked ten years younger than that. He looked prosperous and content and healthy as hell.

But he lived in a house with bars on its windows and a vicious dog prowling its rooms, and sat in a garden with a

plastic bubble over it, and told guests to be sure to lock the gate after they entered. Whether he admitted it to himself or not, he lived in fear—and that is a damned poor way for any man to live.

He swallowed some of his drink, put the glass down on top of my card—deliberately, I thought—and pointed his cigar at me. "Annie says you're here about Harmon Crane."

"That's right."

"Michael Kiskadon hired you, I assume."

"Yes."

"I'm not surprised. Well, sit down. I don't mind talking to you, although I don't see what you or Michael hope to accomplish this long after the fact."

I stayed where I was; I liked the idea of looking down at him. "He wants to know why his father committed suicide," I said.

"Of course he does. So do I."

"I understand your theory is that Crane shot himself because he was no longer able to write."

"Yes. But obviously I have no proof."

"Did he ever communicate to you that he had writer's block?"

"Not in so many words," Yankowski said. "But he hadn't written anything in weeks and it was plain to anyone who knew him that he was despondent about it."

"Did he ever mention suicide?"

"Not to me. Nor to anyone else I know of."

"So you were surprised when you found him dead that night."

"Surprised? Yes and no. I told you, he was despondent and we were all worried about him."

"This despondence . . . it came on all of a sudden, didn't it?"

"No, it was a gradual thing. Did someone tell you otherwise?"

"Kiskadon seems to think his father was all right up until a few weeks before his death."

34

"Nonsense," Yankowski said. "Who told him that?"

"He didn't say."

"Well, it wasn't that way at all. I told you, Harmon's mental deterioration was gradual. He'd been having trouble working for more than three months."

"Had he been drinking heavily for that long?"

"More or less. Harmon was always fond of liquor, and he always turned to it when there was a crisis in his life. The writer's favorite crutch. Or it was in those days, before drugs became fashionable."

"You seem pretty positive about all this, Counselor." He shrugged, and I said, "Do you also have a clear memory of the night of Crane's suicide?"

The question didn't faze him. "As clear as anyone's memory can be of a thirty-five-year-old incident," he said. "Do I strike you as senile?"

"On the contrary."

He favored me with a lopsided grin. "Aren't you going to sit down?"

"I'd rather stand. Aren't you going to offer me a drink or one of your cigars?"

"Certainly not."

We watched each other like a couple of old pit bulls. I knew what he was thinking and he knew what I was thinking and yet here we were, putting on polite conventions for each other, pretending to be civilized while we sniffed around and nipped at each other's heels. It was a game he'd play for a while, but not indefinitely. If you cornered him, or if you just bothered him a little too much, he would go straight for your throat.

I said, "About the night of the suicide. Crane called and asked you to come to his house, is that right?"

"It is."

"And he was very upset, barely coherent."

"That's right."

"Drunk?"

"Very."

"What did he say, exactly?"

"Words to the effect that he needed to talk."

"He didn't say about what?"

"No."

"Did he sound suicidal?"

"No. If he had I would have called the police."

"Instead you went over there."

"I did."

"And met Mrs. Crane and Adam Porter."

"Yes. They had just returned from dinner."

"Did they seem worried about Crane?"

"Not unduly. Not until I'd told them of his call."

"Then he hadn't given either of them any indication he might be considering suicide?"

"No."

"What happened after you told Porter and Mrs. Crane about the call?"

"She became upset and called Crane's name. When there was no answer we all went upstairs and found the door to his office locked. We shouted his name several times, and when there was still no response we broke in."

"You and Porter."

"Yes."

"Whose idea was it, to break in?"

"Adam's, I think. Does it matter?"

"I suppose not. Was there anything unusual about the office?"

"Unusual? The man was lying dead across his desk."

"I think you know what I mean, Counselor. Anything that struck you *after* you looked at the body and found the suicide note."

He sighed elaborately. He had put on his courtroom manner like a sweater; I might have been a jury, or maybe a judge. "We were all quite distraught; Amanda, in fact, was close to hysterics. The only thing I remember noticing was that the room reeked of whiskey, which was hardly unusual."

"Had Crane been dead long?"

"Less than an hour," Yankowski said, "according to the best estimate of the police coroner. He must have shot himself within minutes after he telephoned me."

"Why do you suppose he'd call you to come talk to him and then almost immediately shoot himself?"

He gave me a reproachful look. "You've been a detective almost as many years as I practiced law," he said. "Suicides are unstable personalities, prone to all manner of unpredictable behavior. You know that as well as I do."

"Uh-huh. Were you a close friend of Crane's, Counselor?"

"Not really. Our relationship was mostly professional."

"Then why did he call *you* that night? Why not someone close to him?"

Yankowski shrugged. "Harmon had no close friends; he was an intensely private man. I think he called me because I represented stability—an authority figure, the voice of reason. I think he wanted to be talked out of killing himself. But his personal demons, coupled with whiskey, drove him to it anyway. He simply couldn't make himself wait."

There wasn't anything to say to that; it sounded reasonable enough. So I said, "I understand you met Crane while he was researching a book."

"That's right. He sat through a narcotics trial at which I was assistant defense counsel—a similar case to one in a novel he was writing at the time—and we struck up an acquaintance."

"How did you happen to become his attorney?"

"A short time after we met, a woman in Menlo Park began harassing him, claiming he had stolen her idea for one of his early Johnny Axe novels—I don't remember which one. Nothing came of it; I persuaded her to drop her notion of a plagiarism suit."

"I'll bet you did. What was her name, do you remember?"

"Tinklehoff. Maude Tinklehoff. No one could forget a name like that."

"Did she make any other trouble for Crane?"

"I hardly think so. She was in her late sixties and suffering from cancer; I believe she died a short time after my dealings with her."

"How long before his suicide was this plagiarism business?"

"At least two years. Perhaps three."

"Did you ever do any other legal work for him?"

"I drew up his will."

"Uh-huh. Who got the bulk of his estate?"

"His wife, of course."

"You mean Amanda Crane."

"Certainly."

"Did he happen to leave *you* anything?"

This question didn't faze him either. "Nothing at all."

"Did he leave anything to either of his ex-wives?"

"No. He wasn't on speaking terms with Michael's mother, Susan, and he had long since fallen out of touch with his first wife."

"Ellen Corneal."

"I believe that was her name, yes."

"Did you know her?"

"No. Nor Susan, if that's your next question."

"Do you know what happened to Ellen Corneal?"

"I have no idea."

"Amanda Crane seems to think her husband was married just once before him," I said, "to Kiskadon's mother. Why do you suppose that is?"

He frowned at me around the nub of his cigar. "How do you know what Amanda Crane thinks?"

"I spoke to her this morning in Berkeley."

For some reason that made him angry. He came bouncing up out of his chair and leaned his face to within a couple of inches of mine and breathed the odors of bourbon and tobacco at me. I stood my ground; I wasn't about to back down from the likes of Yank-'Em-Out Yankowski, bad breath or no bad breath.

38

"I don't like the idea of you bothering her," he said.

"Why should my seeing Mrs. Crane concern you?"

"She's a sick woman. Mentally disturbed."

"So I gathered. But if you're so worried about her, how come *you* haven't been to see her in years?"

"That is my business."

"The reason wouldn't be that she turned you down when you proposed to her, would it?"

His eyes went all funny, hot and cold at the same time, like flames frozen in ice. He put his free hand against my chest and shoved, hard enough to stagger me a little. "Get out of here," he said in a low, dangerous voice. "And don't come back."

I stayed where I was for a time. I was afraid if I moved it would be in his direction, and taking a poke at a seventy-year-old shyster lawyer in his own back yard would be a prize-winning act of stupidity.

"I told you to get off my property. *Now!*"

"My pleasure, Counselor."

I put my back to him and went out through the gate, leaving it wide open behind me. Inside the house I could hear the dog making growling noises, but they weren't as vicious as the ones I'd just heard from Yankowski. Pit bull—yeah. Sniff around, sniff around, and then right for the throat.

Whatever that thing in the house was, its master was a far nastier son of a bitch.

FIVE

Kerry and I were having dinner when the earthquake happened.

It was a little after six-thirty and we were in a cozy Italian

place that we both liked—Piombo's, out on Taraval near Nineteenth Avenue. San Francisco's best restaurants aren't downtown or at Fisherman's Wharf or in any of the other districts that cater to tourists; where you find them is in the neighborhoods, residential and otherwise. The chef at Piombo's makes eggplant parmigiana and veal saltimbocca to rival any in North Beach, and at two bucks less a plate.

We had just ordered—the eggplant for Kerry, the veal for me—and we were working on our drinks and I was telling her about my new case. I hadn't told her yet about dinner tomorrow night with Eberhardt and Wanda; I was waiting until her stomach was full, because I figured then she'd be less inclined to throw something at me. As it was, she was in a twitchy mood: one of those days in the advertising business— she worked as a copywriter for the Bates and Carpenter agency—that "make you want to get up on a table and start screaming," as she'd put it.

Her drink was a martini, which was a good indicator of just how wired she was; she seldom drank anything stronger than white wine. She had already knocked most of it back, to good effect: she wasn't nervously toying with her olive anymore and her face looked less tense in the candlelight. Piombo's is an old-fashioned place with big, dim chandeliers and gilt-framed mirrors and one stone-faced wall full of niches stuffed with wine bottles; the candles are not only romantic but necessary if you want to see what you're eating.

Candlelight does nice things for most people's features, and it does especially nice things for Kerry's. Puts little fiery glints in her auburn hair. Makes her chameleon green eyes shine darkly and her mouth look even softer and sexier than it is. Subtracts ten years from her age, not that forty is an unattractive age and not that she needs those years subtracted. Handsome lady, my lady. I wouldn't have traded her for five Hollywood starlets, Princess Diana, and a beauty queen to be named later.

She was sitting with one elbow on the table and her chin propped on that hand, giving me her rapt attention. My busi-

ness always interested her—too damned much sometimes, as I had cause to rue—and she found the Harmon Crane matter particularly intriguing because of the pulp angle. Like Crane, both of her parents had been pulp writers. Ivan Wade had written horror stories—still did—and as far as I was concerned, was something of a horror himself. Cybil Wade, surprisingly enough for an angelic little woman with a sweet smile, had produced a substantial number of very good *Black Mask*-style private eye yarns under the male pseudonym of Samuel Leatherman.

So there we were, Kerry with her martini and me with my one alloted beer, discussing Harmon Crane while we waited for our minestrone. I was just about to ask her if she thought her folks might have known Crane—and then the shaking started.

It wasn't much at the beginning; and my first thought was that one of the big Muni Metro trains was rumbling by outside, because Piombo's is on the L Taraval streetcar line and you can sometimes feel the vibrations of the Metros' passage. But instead of diminishing after a couple of seconds, the tremors gathered intensity. Kerry said, "Earthquake?" and I said, "Yeah," and we just sat there. So did everybody else in the room, all of us poised, diners at their tables, a few people on stools at the bar, the barman and the waiters and waitresses in various freeze-frame poses—waiting.

The tremors went on and on, still sharpening. Ten seconds, fifteen—each second stretched out so that it seemed like a full minute. Silverware clattered on the tables; glasses hopped, spilling beer out of mine and knocking somebody else's off onto the floor with a dull crash. The chandeliers were swaying; the gilt mirrors quivered and leaned drunkenly; the wine bottles in their wall niches made jumpy rattling noises. The flickering of the candle flames gave the room an eerie, unstable look, as if we were all inside a giant box that was being rocked from side to side.

But this was a very San Francisco crowd: natives and long-time residents who had been through earthquakes before

41

and were conditioned to them. Nobody panicked, nobody went charging out into the streets yelling like Chicken Little. The people sitting under the chandeliers and in the shadows of the mirrors got up and backed off; the rest of us just sat still, waiting, not saying anything. Except for the rattling and rumbling of inanimate objects, it was as still as a tomb in there.

What seemed like a long time passed before the tremors began to subside; I had no idea how long until the media announced it later. I thought the biggest of the mirrors was going to break loose and fall, and it might have if the quake had gone on any longer; as it was, nothing fell off the walls or off the tables except that one glass. When the tremors finally quit altogether, a kind of rippling sigh went through the room—a release of tension that was both audible and palpable. The people who were on their feet sat down again. The barman moved; the waiters and waitresses moved. A woman laughed nervously. Everybody began talking at once, not just among their own little groups but to others in the room. A man said in a loud voice, "Big one—five point five at least," and the mustachioed barman called back in jovial tones, "*Voto contrario, signore! Sei à cinque!* Six point five!" It was as if we were all old friends at some sort of festive party. An earthquake has that effect on strangers in public places: it creates the same kind of brief camaraderie, in a small way at least, that the survivors of the London Blitz must have felt.

Kerry said, "Wow," and drank the rest of her martini. But she didn't look unnerved; if anything, the quake seemed to have put an end to her twitchiness and given her a subdued aspect. I didn't feel unnerved either. That is another thing about earthquakes: when you've experienced enough of them, even the bigger ones like this no longer frighten you. All you feel while they're happening is a kind of numb helplessness, because in your mind is the thought that maybe this is the Big One, the one that knocks down buildings and kills hundreds if not thousands of people. And when they end, and you and your surroundings are still in one piece, you find yourself

thinking, No big deal, just another quake, and all you feel then is relief. There is little or no lingering worry. Worrying about earthquakes is like worrying about some damn-fool politician starting a nuclear war: all it does is make you a little crazy.

The guy at the next table asked me if I thought there'd be any aftershocks and I said I didn't know. The barman already had the TV over the back bar turned on and was flipping channels to catch the first news reports—epicenter of the quake, the damage it had done, how high it had measured on the Richter scale at the Berkeley seismology lab. Two guys across the room were making bets, one saying it had been over six and the other wagering under six. That sort of thing seemed a little ghoulish at this point, with the severity of the quake still in doubt, but it was understandable enough: a right of survival.

Kerry and I talked a little, not much, while things got back to normal around us; the thirty-five-year-old suicide of a pulp writer didn't seem quite so interesting or important at the moment. One of the waitresses brought our minestrone. The shakeup hadn't had any effect on my appetite, except maybe to sharpen it. The same was true with Kerry, and apparently with everyone else in Piombo's. We put the minestrone away with gusto, along with a couple of slices of bread each, even though I hadn't been going to have any bread on account of my semi-diet, and our entrees were being served when the barman called out to someone in the kitchen, "Hey, Dino! *Sei à due! Minuto secondo trenta-sette.* I told you, didn't I?" and then turned up the volume on the TV set.

We all looked up at the screen. A newscaster was repeating the facts that the quake had measured 6.2 on the Richter scale and had lasted for thirty-seven seconds. Its epicenter was down around Morgan Hill, near San Jose, and it had been felt as far north as Fort Bragg, as far east as Lake Tahoe. There were scattered reports of property damage, of earth fissures, but no one had been reported killed or badly injured and no structures had collapsed anywhere. There had

been three aftershocks, none above three-point and none felt in San Francisco. A minor quake, really, despite its original magnitude. Nothing to fret about. The Big One was still somewhere in the future, the newscaster said, smiling.

Yeah, I thought. Like that other Big One, death itself.

Which was a morbid thought and I put it out of my head and attacked my veal saltimbocca. It was as good as ever. I had a second beer with it, the hell with my semi-diet, and Kerry had some wine with her eggplant. Neither of us wanted coffee or dessert. All we wanted now was to get out of there, to be alone somewhere; the feeling of camaraderie had evaporated and Piombo's was again a place full of strangers.

On the sidewalk outside Kerry said, "My apartment, okay? If I know Cybil she's already called at least three times. She'll be frantic if I don't phone and tell her I'm all right."

"How come? They have earthquakes in L.A. too."

"Bigger than up here. But she subscribes to the theory that one of these days San Francisco is going to disappear into the Pacific."

"The country would be better off if it was L.A. that disappeared into the Pacific," I said. "Think of all the lousy movies and TV shows that would never get made."

"Hollywood can go," she said, "but not Pasadena." Pasadena was where Cybil and Ivan the Terrible lived. "Come on, we'll make a fire. It's a good night for a fire."

Her apartment is on Diamond Heights, a fashionable newer section of the city whose main attraction is a sweeping view of San Francisco, the Bay, and the East Bay communities. Less than ten seconds after we came in, the telephone rang. "See?" she said. "Cybil—I'll bet you five dollars."

"No bet. When you get done, let me talk to her."

"Why?"

"I want to ask her about Harmon Crane."

She lifted the receiver on the fourth ring, and it was Cybil, all right. Kerry spent the better part of ten minutes reassuring her mother that the earthquake hadn't done her or her possessions any harm. I suppose that was how the conver-

sation went, anyway; I quit paying much attention after the first fifteen seconds. I considered turning on the TV, to see if there were other news bulletins, and decided I didn't really want to hear any more tonight about the quake. Instead I went and got a Pine Mountain log and put it on the grate in the fireplace. I was hunting around for some matches when Kerry finished talking and called me to the phone.

Cybil was in one of her manic, chatty moods; it took me a couple of minutes to introduce the topic of Harmon Crane, to ask her if she'd known him.

"Not really," she said. "I met him once, at a publishing party in New York—the late forties, I think. Why on earth are you asking about Harmon Crane? He's been dead . . . my God, it must be more than thirty years."

"Thirty-five years," I said. "He committed suicide."

"Yes, that's right. He shot himself."

"You wouldn't have any idea why, would you?"

"The usual reasons writers do away with themselves, I suppose," she said wryly. "Why are you so interested?"

I told her about Michael Kiskadon and the reason he'd hired me. Then I asked, "Would Ivan have known Crane any better than you?"

"I doubt it. Do you want me to put him on?"

"Uh, no, that's all right." Ivan and I didn't get along; in fact, we hated each other a little. He thought I was too old and too coarse for Kerry, and in a dangerous and unstable and slightly shady profession. I thought he was a pompous, overbearing jerk. A conversation with him, even on the telephone, was liable to degenerate into a sniping match, if not something worse, and that would only get Kerry upset. "Do you know anyone who might have been friendly with Crane back in 1949? Any other pulp writer, for instance?"

"Well . . . have you talked to Russ Dancer?"

"Dancer? He didn't move to California until 1950, did he?"

"Not permanently. But he lived in San Francisco off and

on during 1949—I'm sure he did. He's still living up there somewhere, isn't he?"

"Redwood City. As of last Christmas, anyway."

"Well, he might have known Crane. I can't think of anyone else. Ivan and I did't know many people in the San Francisco area back then."

"Just out of curiosity—what was your impression of Crane the one time you met him?"

"Oh, I liked him. He was funny in a silly sort of way, very much like his books and pulp stories. He drank a lot, but then we all did in those days."

I thanked her and we said our good-byes. Dancer, huh? I thought as I put the receiver back into its cradle. I had crossed paths with Russell Dancer twice in the past six years, once on a case in Cypress Bay down the coast and once here in San Francisco, at the same pulp magazine convention where I'd met Kerry and her parents. Dancer had managed to get himself arrested for murder at that convention, and I had proved him innocent and earned his slavish and undying gratitude. Or so he'd claimed when the police let him out of jail. That had been two years ago and I hadn't seen him since; had only had a couple of scrawled Christmas cards, one from Santa Cruz and the other from Redwood City, some twenty-five miles down the Peninsula.

The prospect of seeing Dancer again was not a particularly pleasing one, which was the reason I hadn't bothered to look *him* up. Dancer was a wasted talent, a gifted writer who had taken the easy road into hackwork thirty-odd years ago and who still cranked out pulp for the current paperback markets—adult Westerns, as of our last meeting. He was also a self-hating alcoholic with a penchant for trouble and a deep, bitter, and unrequited love for Cybil Wade. A little of him went a long way. Still, if there was a chance he had known Harmon Crane, it would be worth getting in touch with him. Assuming I could find him, in Redwood City or elsewhere: he moved around a lot, mostly to keep ahead of the IRS and his creditors.

I swung away from the telephone table. Kerry was standing by the sliding glass doors to the balcony, her arms folded under her breasts, looking out at the lights of the city and the East Bay. I said her name, but she didn't turn right away. And when she did turn she gazed at me for a few seconds, an odd expression on her face, before she spoke.

"It's cold in here," she said.

"Is it? Well, I'll light the fire—"

"No, don't."

"Why not?"

"Let's go to bed," she said.

"Bed? It's not even nine o'clock. . . ."

"Don't be dense," she said.

"Oh," I said.

"Now. Right away."

"Big hurry, huh?"

She came over and took hold of my arm. Her eyes were bright with the sudden urgency. "Right *now,*" she said, and pulled me toward the bedroom.

It wasn't that she was hot for me; it wasn't even sex, really. It was a belated reaction to the quake—a need to be close to someone, to reaffirm life, after having faced all that potentially destructive force. Earthquakes have that effect on people too, sometimes.

SIX

The morning *Chronicle* was full of quake news, not that that was surprising. I seldom read the papers anymore—I have to deal with enough bad news on a daily basis without compounding it—but my curiosity got the better of me in this case; so I skimmed through the various reports while I was having coffee and waiting for Kerry to get dressed.

There was more damage than originally estimated, though none of it involving major loss or casualties. Some mobile homes had been knocked off their foundations down in Morgan Hill, and a freeway overpass in San Ramon had suffered some structural ruin. Out along the coast, especially in West Marin, several earth cracks had been opened up, one of them fifty yards long and three feet wide on a·cattle graze belonging to an Olema dairy rancher. He claimed one of his cows had been swallowed up by the break, even though it wasn't very deep and there was no physical evidence to support his contention. "For all I know," he was quoted as saying, "that cow's all the way over in China by now."

I got a chuckle out of that, and so did Kerry when I read it to her. The lighter side of a grim subject.

Before we left her apartment, I girded myself and told her about dinner with Eberhardt and Wanda. She didn't say anything for fifteen seconds or so, just looked at me the way she does, and I was certain I was in for a little verbal abuse; but Kerry is nothing if not unpredictable. She just sighed and said, "What time?"

"I don't know yet. I'll call you after I talk to Eb."

"God, the things I do for you."

"Come on, babe, it won't be so bad."

"That's what you said last time."

"Was last time really so bad?"

"Was the Spanish Inquisition really so bad?"

"Well, I admit it did rack up a few people."

She glared at me, cracked me on the arm, said, "You and your puns," and then burst out laughing. Another potential disaster averted.

I followed her Mustang down off Twin Peaks and then detoured up Franklin and over to my flat on Pacific Heights. In a burst of energy last weekend, Kerry had forced me to help her clean the place up; it was spic and span, no dust mice nesting under the furniture, no dust clinging chummily to my shelved collection of some 6,500 pulps, which covered two full walls. It didn't look right and it didn't feel right. The home of

an unrepentant slob ought to have some *dust* in it, for God's sake, if not a scatter of dirty dishes. Neatness depresses me.

I went over to the secretary desk in the corner and rummaged around in one of the drawers until I found the box full of old Christmas cards. Dancer's was on the bottom, naturally. I copied down his Redwood City address, guessing at one numeral and a couple of letters in the street name—Dancer had never won any awards for penmanship. In the bedroom I pawed through the bookcase where I keep my modest collection of hardcovers and paperbacks. I used to pile them up in the closet, on the shelves and on the floor, but they fell over on me one day when I opened the door, in a kind of Fibber McGee chain reaction; when I got done cursing I went out and bought the bookcase. It takes me a long time to learn a lesson sometimes, but then it damned well stays learned.

I had only two of Harmon Crane's Johnny Axe novels—the first, *Axe Marks the Spot,* and *Axe of Mercy.* It had been a while since I'd read either one, and it seemed like a good idea to refamiliarize myself with his work when time permitted. I tucked the two books under my arm and went back into the nice, neat living room. And right out of it again. It was lonely in there, now that Kerry had murdered all my old friends, the dust mice.

Eberhardt wasn't in yet when I got to the office; he seldom shows up before nine-thirty and sometimes not until ten. I opened the window behind his desk to get rid of the stale smell of his pipe, after which I filled the coffeepot from the bottle of Alhambra water and put it on the hotplate. Morning ritual. I completed it by checking the answering machine and discovering—lo!—that there weren't any messages.

I sat down and rang up San Mateo County information and asked the operator if there was a listing for Russell Dancer. There wasn't. Damn. Now I would have to drive all the way down to Redwood City, on what might well be a wild goose chase. The way Dancer moved around, one hop and two skips ahead of his creditors and the IRS, he could be

somewhere else in California by now. Like in an alcoholic ward, or maybe even in jail. With Dancer, anything was possible.

Well, I had one other lead to follow up first: Stephen Porter, Amanda Crane's friend. I dialed the number I'd copied out of the directory yesterday, and this time I got an answer. The right one, too, for a change. A scratchy male voice, punctuated by coughs and wheezes, informed me that yes, he was Adam Porter's brother and yes, he would be willing to talk to me, either before eleven or possibly after three, though he might be busy then, because he had classes between those two times, not to mention lunch, heh, heh (which was either a feeble chuckle or some sort of nasal gasp). I said I could come over right away and he said fine and gave me the address. After which he hacked again in my ear, loud enough to make me wince, and hung up.

The telephone rang almost immediately after I cradled the handset. Michael Kiskadon, bubbling over with eagerness and curiosity. How was my investigation going? Had I found out anything yet? Who had I talked to? Who was I going to talk to? I gave him a brief verbal report, assured him I would be in touch as soon as I had something definite to report, and told him I had an appointment to get him off the line. But I had a feeling I'd be hearing from him again before long. He was that kind of client, and clients like that can be a pain in the ass.

Eberhardt breezed in just as I was about to leave. He was all smiles this morning, chipper and cheerful and whistling a spritely tune. "Coffee," he said, sniffing. "Man, can I use some of that."

"Big night, huh?"

"Yeah, well," he said, and smirked at me.

"You not only got laid last night," I said, "you got laid this morning. Not more than an hour ago, in fact. You had to hurry getting dressed so you wouldn't be any later than you usually are."

He gawped at me. "How the hell did you deduce all of that, Sherlock?"

"Your fly's still open," I said.

North Beach used to be a quiet, predominately Italian neighborhood, the place you went when you wanted pasta, Chianti, a game of bocce, conversation about *la dolce vita* and *il patria d'Italia,* the company of mustachioed waiters in gondolier costumes singing arias from operas by Puccini and Verdi. Not anymore. There are still Italians in North Beach, and you can still get the pasta and Chianti and conversation, if not the bocce and the singing waiters; but their turf has been reduced to a mere pocket, and the vitality and Old World atmosphere are little more than memories.

The Chinese are partly responsible, having gobbled up North Beach real estate when Chinatown, to the west, began to burst its boundaries. Another culprit is the so-called beatnik or Bohemian element that took over upper Grant Avenue in the fifties, paving the way for the hippies and the introduction of drugs in the sixties, which in turn paved the way for the jolly current mix of motorcycle toughs, aging hippies, coke and hash dealers, and the pimps and small-time crooks who work the flesh palaces along lower Broadway. Those topless and bottomless "Silicone Alley" nightclubs, made famous by Carol Doda in the late sixties, also share responsibility: they had added a smutty leer to the gaiety of North Beach and turned the heart of it into a ghetto.

Parts of the neighborhood, particulary those up around Coit Tower, where the Cranes had once lived, are still desirable, and in the shrunken Italian pocket you can still get a sense of what it was like in the old days. But most of the flavor is gone. North Beach is tasteless now, and hard and vague and unpleasant—like a week-old mostaccioli made without spices or garlic. And that is another thing that is all but gone: twenty-five years ago you couldn't get within a thousand yards of North Beach without picking up the fine,

rich fragrance of garlic. Nowadays, you're much more likely to smell fried egg roll and the sour stench of somebody's garbage.

Stephen Porter's studio was on Vallejo Street, half a block off upper Grant. It was an old building, the entrance to which was down a narrow alleyway plastered with No Parking signs. A hand-lettered card over the topmost of three bells read: *1A—Stephen Porter, Sculptor.* And below that: *Lessons Available.*

I rang the bell and pretty soon the door lock buzzed. I went into a dark hallway with a set of stairs on the right and a cat sitting on the bottom step giving me the once-over. I said, "Hello, cat," and it said, "Maurrr," politely, and began to lick its shoulder. The hallway ran past the stairs, deeper into the building; at the far end of it, a door opened and a man poked his head out. "Down here," he said.

I went down there. "Mr. Porter?"

"Yes, that's right. You're the gentleman who called? The detective?"

I said I was, and he bobbed his head, coughed, wheezed a little, and let me come in. He was about sixty, a little guy with not much hair and delicate, almost womanish hands. The hands were spotted with dried clay; so was the green smock he wore. There was even a spot of clay on the knot of his spiffy red bow tie.

The room he led me into was a single, cavernous enclosure, brightly lit by flourescent ceiling tubes, that looked as if it had been formed by knocking out some walls. Along one side was a raised platform piled high with finished sculptures, most of them fanciful animals and birds. At the rear was a curtained-off area, probably Porter's living quarters. The rest of the space was cluttered with clay-smeared tables, a trio of potter's wheels complete with foot treadles, drums full of pre-mixed clay, and some wooden scaffolding to hold newly formed figures while they dried. Spread out and bunched up on the floor were several pieces of canvas, all of them caked with dried spatters of clay. But they hadn't caught all of the

droppings, not by any means: what I could see of the bare wood underneath was likewise splotched.

"There aren't any chairs out here, I'm afraid," Porter said. "We can go in back, if you prefer. . . ."

"This is fine. I won't take up much of your time."

"Well," he said, and then turned away abruptly and did some more coughing and hacking, followed by a series of squeaky wheezes. When he had his breath back he said, "Emphysema." And immediately produced a package of Camels from the pocket of his smock and fired up.

I stared at him. "If you've got emphysema," I said, "why not quit smoking?"

"Too late for that," he said with a sort of philosophical resignation. "My lungs are already gone. I'll probably be dead in another year or two anyway."

The words gave me a chill. A few years back, when I was a two-pack-a-day smoker myself, I had developed a lesion on one lung and spent too many sleepless nights worrying that maybe *I'd* be dead in another year or two. The lesion had turned out to be benign, but I still hadn't had a cigarette since. It was a pact I'd made with whatever forces controlled the universe; and so far they had kept their end of the bargain by allowing me to go on living without medical complications.

I said, "I'm sorry, Mr. Porter," and I meant it.

He shrugged. "Weak lungs and frail bodies run in my family," he said. "My brother Adam died of lung cancer, you know."

"No, I didn't know."

"Yes. He was only fifty-four." Porter sucked in smoke, coughed it out, and said wheezily, "You're interested in Harmon Crane. May I ask why?"

"His son hired me to find out why he shot himself."

"His son? I didn't know Harmon had a son."

"Neither did he." I went on to explain about Michael Kiskadon and his purpose in hiring me.

Porter said, "I see. Well, I don't know that I can help you. Adam knew Harmon much better than I did."

53

"But you *were* acquainted with him?"

"Oh yes. I was very young and impressed by his success. I used to badger Adam to take me along whenever he got together with the Cranes."

"How did Crane feel about that?"

"He didn't seem to mind. At least, not until the last few weeks of his life. Then he wouldn't deal with anyone."

"Do you have any idea what caused his depression?"

"Not really. But it was right after he returned from Tomales Bay that we all noticed it."

"Oh? What was he doing at Tomales Bay?"

"He had a little retreat, a cabin; he went there when he was having trouble working in the city."

"Went there alone, you mean?"

"Yes. He liked solitude."

"How long did he usually stay?"

"Oh, a couple of weeks at the most."

"How long was he there that last time?"

"I'm not sure. A week or so, I think. He came back the day after the earthquake."

"Earthquake?"

Porter nodded. "I might have forgotten about that, if it hadn't been for the one last night. The quake in '49 was just about as severe, centered somewhere up north, and it did some minor damage in the Tomales Bay area. Harmon had a terror of earthquakes; he used to say that was the only thing he hated about living in San Francisco. Adam thought the quake might have had something to do with Harmon's depression, but I don't see how that's possible."

"Neither do I. Did Crane say anything about his experience out at Tomales?"

"Not to my knowledge."

"Not even to his wife? Didn't she talk to him after it happened? On the telephone, I mean."

"Well, he did call her briefly to tell her he was all right. But that was all. And he wouldn't talk about it after he returned to the city."

"How did Mrs. Crane feel about his trips to Tomales? Didn't she mind him going away alone like that?"

"No. Amanda was always very . . . passive, I suppose is the word. Whatever Harmon did was fine with her." Porter paused, fought down another cough, and ground out his cigarette in a hollowed-out lump of clay. "You've talked to her? Amanda?"

"For a few minutes yesterday."

"About Harmon's death?"

"No. She wouldn't discuss it."

"It's just as well. She . . . well, she had a severe breakdown, you know, after Adam and that shyster, Yankowski, found the body. She hasn't been right in the head since."

"So I gathered. She asked about you, Mr. Porter."

"Did she?" A kind of softness came into his face; he smiled faintly. "I suppose she wonders why I haven't been to see her the past few months."

"Yes. She said she'd like to see you again."

He sighed, and it turned into another cough. "Well, I suppose I'll have to go then. I stopped the visits because they depress me. Seeing her the way she is . . ." He shook his head. "She was such a vital woman before the shooting. An attractive, vital, happy woman."

He was in love with her too, I thought. At least a little. She must have been quite a woman before the night of December 10, 1949.

I said, "Crane's little retreat at Tomales—do you recall where it was?"

"No, not exactly. I never went there. Adam did, once, at Harmon's invitation; it seems to me he said it was on the east shore. But I can't be sure."

"Did Crane own the place?"

"I believe he leased it."

"Would you have any idea who from?"

"Well, as a matter of fact, I would. An Italian fellow in Tomales. The town, I mean. Harmon used his name in one of his Johnny Axe books, made him the villain. He liked to do

things like that—inside jokes, he called them. He had a puckish sense of humor."

"Was the Italian a realtor?"

"No, I don't think so. A private party."

"What was his name?"

Porter did some cudgeling of his memory. But then he shook his head again and said, "I just don't remember."

"The title of the book?"

"Nor that. I read all of them when they were published, but I haven't looked at one in years. I believe I stored them away with Adam's books after he died." Porter paused again, musingly this time. "You know," he said, "there was a box of Harmon's papers among my brother's effects."

"Papers?"

"Literary papers—manuscripts, letters, and so on. I don't know how Adam came to have them; probably through Amanda. If you think they might be of help, I'll see if I can find the box. It's somewhere down in the basement."

"I'd appreciate that, Mr. Porter. You never know what might prove useful."

"I'll start looking this evening."

"Can you give me the names of any other friends of Crane's I should talk to?"

"I didn't really know any of Harmon's friends," he said. "I don't believe he had many. He spent most of his time writing or researching. Have you talked to Yankowski yet?"

"Yes. He wasn't very helpful."

"I'm not surprised. An unpleasant sort. I don't know why Harmon dealt with him."

"How did your brother feel about Yankowski?"

"The same as I do. He found him overbearing. And the way he pestered poor Amanda after Harmon's death . . ."

"Pestered her how?"

"He wanted to marry her. That was before he found out her mind was permanently damaged, of course."

"He left her alone after he found out?"

"Fortunately, yes."

There didn't seem to be anything more to ask Porter; I waited while he lighted another Camel and got done coughing, thanked him for his time, and started for the door. But he wasn't quite ready to let go of *me* yet. He tagged along, with his face scrunched up thoughtfully again and his breath making funny little rattling noises in his throat.

When we got to the door he said, "There is one thing. I don't know that I ought to bring it up, after all this time, but . . . well, it's something that has bothered me for thirty-five years. Bothered Adam, too, while he was alive."

"What is it, Mr. Porter?"

"The circumstances of Harmon's death. They just didn't seem right."

"How do you mean?"

"Well . . . in the first place, it's very hard to believe that he would have killed himself, even in a state of severe depression. If you'd known Harmon you'd understand. He wasn't a courageous man; he feared death more than most of us."

I frowned at him. "Are you suggesting his death might not have been suicide?"

"I'm suggesting that it is a possibility."

"Who had reason to want him dead?"

"No one that I know of. Or that Adam knew of. That was one of the reasons the police discounted the idea when Adam broached it to them."

"What were the other reasons?"

"The main one was the locked office door. They said there was no way anyone but Harmon could have locked it from the inside. But that door was exactly what bothered us the most."

"Why?"

"Harmon never locked doors, not even the front door to his house; he was a trusting man and he was forever misplacing things like keys. Besides, he was alone in the house that night. Why would a man alone in his own home lock his office door, even if he *did* intend to take his own life?"

I didn't say anything.

57

"You see?" Porter said. "It *could* have been murder, couldn't it?"

SEVEN

When I left North Beach I drove over to the foot of Clay Street and got onto the freeway interchange, heading south for Redwood City. As I drove I mulled over what Porter had told me. Not suicide—murder. Well, it was a possibility, as he'd said; and it would make an intriguing mystery out of Crane's death. But the police had determined that there was no way for a locked-room gimmick to have been worked, and I had a healthy respect for the SFPD Homicide Detail; I knew a lot of the men who'd been on it over the years, from my own days on the cops and from my friendship with Eberhardt, who had worked that detail for a decade and a half as inspector and then lieutenant. No, if they'd felt Crane's death was suicide, then it must have been suicide. And never mind why he decided to lock the office door before he put his .22 Browning against his temple and pulled the trigger. He'd been drunk at the time, depressed and overwrought; a man in that condition is liable to commit any sort of irrational act.

Sure, I thought, sure. But all the same I wanted a look at the police report—if it still existed and if Eberhardt could find it. Even the best of cops makes mistakes now and then, just like the rest of us.

It was a little past noon when I reached the Redwood City exit off 101. For the San Mateo county seat, it's a quiet little town sprawled out on both sides of El Camino Real and the Southern Pacific Railroad tracks. Not nearly as affluent as Atherton and Palo Alto to the south, or Burlingame and

Hillsborough to the north. Just a town like a lot of other towns, with a fair amount of low-income housing along tree-shaded streets. A few writers had lived there over the years, some of whom had written for the pulps. I wondered if any of those were still alive and if Russ Dancer knew them. And if he did, if he had anything in common with them after all these years.

I pulled into a Chevron station near Broadway, the main downtown arterial. And pumped my own gas while a fat, indolent teenager looked on, waiting to take my money. Self-service at gas stations is one of my pet peeves. High prices, and you do all the work yourself. What the hell did attendants like this one do to earn their salary? Not much, that was for damned sure. Instead of walking over to where he was, I got back into the car so that *he* had to move his fat in order to get paid. Small satisfaction, but you take your satisfactions where you can these days.

I took another one by sitting there at the pump for an extra couple of minutes while I dug a Redwood City street map out of the bag of maps in the glove compartment and looked up Stambough Street, Dancer's last known address. Only it *wasn't* Stambough, it was Stambaugh: I had mistaken an *a* for an *o* in the scrawled return address on Dancer's Christmas card envelope. Stambaugh Street was only a few blocks from where I was, not far off Broadway—more or less downtown and more or less close to the SP tracks.

But I didn't go there directly after I left the nonservice station. I stopped instead on Broadway and went into the first café I saw to eat lunch. I was hungry, and Dancer isn't somebody you want to deal with on an empty stomach.

I took my copies of *Axe Marks the Spot* and *Axe of Mercy* with me, and skimmed through them while I ate. Neither one had an Italian villain in it. I couldn't recall which of the others did have; it had been too long since I'd read them. I would have to go see Kiskadon later on and check through his copies.

With a cheese omelette and a glass of iced tea under my

belt, I drove to Stambaugh Street. The number I wanted turned out to be a somewhat seedy rooming house near a block-long thrift store: a sprawling, two-story Victorian with turrets and gables and brick chimneys, all badly in need of paint and general repair. Two sickly palm trees grew in a front yard enclosed by a picket fence with a fourth of the pickets broken or missing altogether. Nice place. Every time I crossed paths with Dancer, he seemed to have tumbled a little further downhill.

I parked in front and went through the gate and up onto the creaky front porch. There was only one entrance and no marked mailboxes to identify who lived there. Just a doorbell button and a small card above it that said ROOM FOR RENT— SEE MANAGER. I tried the door, found it locked, and pushed the bell. Pretty soon somebody buzzed me into a dark hallway that smelled of Lysol and, curiously, popcorn. The somebody—a woman—was leaning out of a doorway beyond a flight of stairs, giving me a squint-eyed look.

I went over to her. The door was marked MANAGER and the woman was about fifty, gray-haired, wearing sequin-rimmed glasses. She had a face like something in an old, discolored wallpaper pattern—the gargoyle kind.

"Something I can do for you?" Brillo-pad voice, like Lauren Bacall with a sore throat.

"I'm looking for a man named Russell Dancer."

Her mouth got all quirky with what I took to be disgust. "Him," she said. "You wouldn't be a cop, would you?"

"I wouldn't. Why?"

"You look like a cop. Dancer's been in jail before."

"In Redwood City, you mean?"

"Sure. He been in jail somewhere else too?"

He had, but I wasn't about to tell her that. "What was he arrested for?"

"Drunk and disorderly, what else? You a bill collector?"

"No."

"Process server?"

"No. He *does* still live here?"

"Yeah, he lives here. But he won't much longer if he don't start payin his rent on time. He's just like my ex—a deadbeat and a bum. This was *my* house, I'd throw him out on the fuckin street."

"Uh-huh."

"Right out on the fuckin street," she said.

"What's his room number?"

"Six. Upstairs."

"He in now?"

She shrugged. "Who knows? If he ain't you can probly find him at Mama Luz's, over on Main. That's where he does his drinkin when he don't do it here."

"Thanks."

"Don't mention it. You a friend of his?"

"Religious advisor."

"What?"

"His religious advisor. I'm teaching him how to love his neighbor. Maybe you'd like a few lessons too."

"Fuckin wise guy," she said, and shut the door in my face.

I went upstairs, found the door with the numeral 6 on it, and whacked it a couple of times with the heel of my hand. Nobody answered. On impulse I tried the knob: Dancer had forgotten to lock it, or just hadn't bothered. I poked my head inside. Just a room, not much in the way of furnishings; clothing strewn around, an empty half-gallon jug of Lucky Stores generic bourbon, a scatter of secondhand paperbacks that had probably come out of the thrift store nearby. I didn't see any sign of a typewriter or a manuscript or anything else that a professional writer ought to have lying around.

I shut the door and went back downstairs and out into the warm sunshine. It was a nice day down here, cloudless, with not much wind; the Peninsula is usually ten to twenty degrees warmer than San Francisco and this day was no exception. I left my car where it was and hoofed it along Stambaugh to Main Street. Mama Luz's wasn't hard to find. It was half a block to the west, and its full name, spelled out on a

garish neon sign, was Mama Luz's Pink Flamingo Tavern. Some moniker for a sleazy neighborhood bar. I crossed the street, shook my head at the scrawny pink flamingo painted on the front wall, and went through an honest-to-God set of batwing doors.

The interior wasn't any better than the exterior. The usual bar arrangement, some warping wooden booths, a snooker table with a drop light over it, and a mangled jukebox that looked as if it had been mugged: broken glass top, caved-in side, and a big hole punched or kicked in its midsection. I would not have liked to meet the guy who had done all that damage, even if he'd been justified.

There were four people in the place, including an enormous female bartender. Two of the customers were blue-collar types nursing beers; the third was Dancer, down at the far end, draped over a newspaper with a cigarette hanging out of his face and a glass of something that was probably bourbon close at hand. He was reading with his nose about ten inches from the newsprint, squinting through the cigarette smoke as if he might have gone myopic; he was the type who would go on denying that he needed glasses right up to the day he went blind. He didn't notice me at first, as engrossed as he was, so I had a chance to take stock of him a little.

He had changed in the two years since I'd last seen him, and none of it for the better. He was about sixty-five now and looked every year of it: sagging jowls, heavy lines and wrinkles and age spots on his face and neck, a lot more ruptured blood vessels in his cheeks, and a rum-blossom nose W.C. Fields would have admired. There wasn't much left of his dust-colored hair; age spots littered his naked scalp as well. He looked dissipated and rheumy and too thin for his big frame, as if the flesh were hanging on his bones like a scarecrow's tattered clothing. The thought came to me that he was going to die pretty soon, and it gave me a sharp twinge of pity and compassion. He'd screwed up his own life—we all do to one extent or another—but he hadn't had many breaks, either, and very little luck. At sixty-five he deserved better than

a furnished room near a thrift shop, a stool in Mama Luz's Pink Flamingo Tavern, and death staring at him from the bottom of a whiskey glass.

"Hello, Russ," I said.

His head came up and he peered at me blankly for a couple of seconds. Then recognition animated his features, split his mouth into a bleary grin, and he said, "Well, if it isn't the dago shamus! What you doing here?"

"Looking for you."

"Yeah? Christ, it's been what, two years?" He stood up, more or less steadily—he'd had a few but he wasn't drunk—and punched my arm. He seemed genuinely glad to see me. "You lost some weight, paisano. Looking good."

"So are you," I lied.

"Bullshit. Listen, sit down, sit down, have a drink. You've got time for a drink, haven't you?"

"Sure. If you've got time to talk."

"Anything for you, pal, after what you did for me. Hey, Mama Luz! Drag your fat ass down here and meet an old friend of mine."

The enormous female behind the bar waddled our way. She was Mexican; she must have weighed at least three hundred pounds, all of it encased in a tentlike muumuu thing emblazoned with pink flamingos; and she wore so much powder and rouge and makeup that she resembled a mime. She might have been one, too: she didn't say a word, even when Dancer told her who I was. All she did was nod and stand there waiting.

"So what'll you have?" Dancer asked me. "You still just a beer man?"

"Always. Miller Lite, I guess."

"Miller Lite, Mama. Cold one, huh? Give me another jolt too." She went away to get the drinks and Dancer said, "So how'd you track me down?"

"Card you sent me last Christmas."

"Social call or you working?"

"Working. You might be able to help."

63

"Me? How so?"

"The job has to do with a pulp writer named Harmon Crane. Cybil Wade told me you might have known him."

A corner of his mouth twitched. "Little Sweeteyes," he said. He was talking about Cybil, not Crane. "How is she?"

"Fine."

"And that son of a bitch she's married to? Tell me he dropped dead of a coronary, make my day."

"No such luck."

"He'll outlive us all—like Nixon. You still seeing her daughter?"

"We're engaged, more or less."

"Good for you. Tell Sweeteyes I said hello, next time you talk to her. Hell, give her my love." He grinned lop-sidedly and drained what was left in his glass. Still carrying the torch, I thought. He'd carry it right into the grave with him.

"About Harmon Crane, Russ. *Did* you know him?"

"Old Harmie—sure, I knew him. Met him at a writers' lunch the first time I came out here from New York. I'd read his stuff, he'd read mine. We hit it off."

"That was early 1949?"

"Spring, I think. I hadn't made up my mind to move to California yet, but I figured I would if I could find a place I liked. Tried L.A. first; forget it. So I came up to Frisco."

"You get to know Crane well?"

"We palled around a little, got drunk together a couple of times. Even tried collaborating on a pulp story, but that didn't work out. Too much ego on both sides; believe it or not, I had one back then."

"You had reason. You know what I think of Rex Hannigan."

"Yeah. But Hannigan was a second-rate pulp private eye compared to Johnny Axe. You remember the Axe series?"

"I remember."

Dancer chuckled, as if something funny had just tickled his memory. "Harmie had a hell of a sense of humor. Always

good for a laugh. Last book he wrote, Axe gets framed for a murder of a guy that owns a soup company, see, so Harmie called it *Axe-Tailed Soup*. Perfect title, right? But his editor wouldn't let him use it. Too suggestive, she said; some blue-nose out in the Bible Belt might read a dirty double meaning into it and raise a stink. The editor, this shriveled-up old maid named Bangs, Christ you should have seen her, this Bangs broad wants him to come up with another title quick because the production department and the art department are all set to move. So Harmie waits a couple of days and then sends the new title by collect wire, no comment or anything, just one line. What do you think it was?"

"I don't know, what?"

"'How about *A Piece of Axe*,'" Dancer said, and burst out laughing. I laughed with him. "Man, Bangs almost had a shit hemorrhage and Harmie almost got thrown out on his ear. But he figured it was worth it."

"Uh-huh."

"I remember another time," he said, "we were kidding around with titles for mystery novels—you know, trying to see which of us could come up with the worst one using the word *death*. Things like *Death Plays Pattycake* and *Death Gets a Dose of the Clap*. But Harmie won hands down. Best title for a tough-guy mystery I ever heard."

"What was it?"

"*Fuck You, Death.*"

That didn't strike me quite so funny, considering the way Harmon Crane had died, and I didn't laugh much. Not that Dancer noticed; he was too busy reaching for the fresh highball Mama Luz had set in front of him. He suggested we take our drinks to one of the booths, and we did that.

He said as he lit another cigarette, "How come you're interested in Harmie? Christ, he's been dead what . . . thirty-five years? He did the Dutch, you know."

"I know. That's why I'm interested." I explained it to him briefly. "Were you still in San Francisco when it happened?"

"No. I went back to New York the end of September, to tie up some loose ends. I'd finally made up my mind to settle out here, but I didn't make it back to California until early the next year."

"Were you surprised when you heard about Crane's suicide?"

"Yeah, I was. I never figured him for the kind who'd do the Dutch. I mean, he was one funny guy. But then I knew he had problems, a whole pack of 'em."

"What kind of problems?"

"His marriage. That was the big one."

"Oh? I thought he was happily married."

"Who told you that?"

"His widow."

"Yeah, that figures. She always did pretend she was Cinderella and Harmie was some poor schmuck of a Prince Charming."

"What was the trouble between them?"

"They weren't fucking," Dancer said. Leave it to him to choose the most delicate phrasing whenever possible.

"Why not?"

"She didn't like it. An iceberg in the sack."

"Oh," I said.

"Yeah," he said.

"Were they doing anything about it?"

"You mean was she seeing a shrink?"

"Yes."

"Uh-uh. She wouldn't go. Wouldn't discuss the deed with *Harmie*, let alone some stranger."

"No sex at all between them?"

"Not in close to a year, when I knew him."

"Did he talk much about it?"

"Some. When he was looped."

"Was he seeing other women?"

"Harmie? Nah, I doubt it. He wasn't the type."

"A year is a long time to do without sex," I said.

"I used to think so too. Not anymore."

I let that pass. "He must have loved her quite a bit, to put up with that kind of relationship."

"I guess he did." Dancer showed me another of his lop-sided grins. "Love does crazy things to people. Always has, always will."

"What other problems did Crane have?"

"The booze, for one; he put it away like water. And one of his ex-wives was bugging him."

That was news. I asked, "Which one?"

"Some broad he married when he was in college, I forget her name."

"Ellen Corneal."

"If you say so."

"What was she bugging him about?"

"Money, what else? She was broke, she'd heard how well Harmie was doing, she figured he'd float her a loan for past services." Dancer laughed sardonically. "He sure knew how to pick his women."

"Did Crane give her the money?"

"No. Told her to bugger off. But she kept pestering him anyway."

"Was she living in San Francisco at the time?"

"He didn't say. But if she wasn't, she was close by."

"You know anything about her? What she did for a living, whether she was remarried—like that?"

"Nothing. Harmie didn't say much about her."

"How upset was he that she'd shown up in his life again?"

"Not nearly as upset as he was about not getting laid."

"He seem depressed the last time you saw him?"

"Not that I remember."

"Were you in touch with him after you went back to New York?"

"Nah. Dropped him a note but he didn't answer it. Next thing I knew, he was dead."

"You get to know any of his friends while you were out here?"

"Don't recall any."

"But you did meet some of them."

"One or two, I guess."

"His lawyer, Thomas Yankowski?"

"Name doesn't ring a bell."

"Adam Porter? Stephen Porter?"

"No bells there either."

I had run out of questions to ask. I drank some of my beer while Dancer lit yet another cigarette; then I said it had been good talking to him again and that I appreciated his help, and started to slide out of the booth. But he reached over and caught hold of my arm.

"Hey, come on, don't rush off," he said. "You didn't finish your beer."

"I'm working, Russ, remember?"

"Sure, sure, but you've got time for one more, haven't you? For old times' sake? Hell, it's been two years. Who knows how long it'll be till we hoist another one together."

He was a little drunk now, and inclined toward the maudlin; but there was also a kind of pathetic quality in his voice and manner—a tacit reaching out for a little companionship, a little kindness, that I couldn't bring myself to ignore. He was a lot of things, Dancer was, and one of them was lonely. And maybe another was afraid.

I said, "All right—one more. And I'll buy."

I spent another twenty minutes with him, talking about this and that—a rehash of the pulp convention two years ago, mostly, and how grateful he was to me for clearing him of the murder charge. Just before I left him I asked how he was doing these days, how things were in the writing business.

"Hack business, you mean," he said. The sardonic grin again. "It's lousy. Worst I've ever seen it. Too many hacks and not enough free-lance work; they're lined up around the block trying to get an assignment."

"I thought you had a deal to do a bunch of adult Westerns."

"I did but it blew up. Wrote one and the editor hated it,

said I had my history screwed up and didn't know anything about life in the Old West. Some twenty-two-year-old cunt from Bryn Mawr, never been west of Philadelphia, she says *I* don't know anything about the Old West. Jesus Christ, I was writing horse opera before she was born."

"You pick up any other assignments since?"

". . . Not yet, no."

"Then how are you surviving?"

"Social Security. I hit the magic sixty-five a few months ago. It's not much, but it pays the rent and keeps me in booze and cigarettes."

"You're still writing, though?"

"Sure. Always at the mill. Got a few proposals with my agent, a few irons in the fire. And I'm working up an idea for a big paperback suspense thing that might have a shot. It's just that the market is so goddamned tight right now." Shrugging, he lifted his glass and stared into it. "You know how it is," he said.

I thought about his furnished room over on Stambaugh Street, the empty bottle of generic bourbon and the absence of a typewriter or any other tool of the writer's trade. And I thought about what we both knew was staring back at him from the bottom of his glass.

"Yeah," I said. "I know just how it is."

EIGHT

Eberhardt was out when I got back to the office a little past four. But he had left me a note, as he sometimes did; it was lying on top of a manila envelope on my desk blotter. His typing is almost as bad as his handwriting, what with strikeovers and misspellings and a smeary ribbon on his old Remington, but it's at least decipherable.

3 P.M.

Here's the report on the Crane suicide. Not much there, it was cut and dried.

Woman called for you three times, same one as yesterday. Still wouldn't leave her name or tell me what she wanted, just kept saying she'd call back. Does Kerry know about this?

I'm going out on that repo job for Dennison. In case I don't make it back before you leave the name of the restaurant is Il Roccaforte. 2621 San Bruno Ave. Wanda says 7:30 if that's okay with you and Kerry.

I'll be counting the minutes, Eb, I thought, and sighed, and put the note in my pocket. Il Roccaforte. The Stronghold. Some name for a restaurant. It sounded more like an outfit that rented you storage space, or maybe one of those S&M leather bars over on Folsom. Leave it to Wanda to pick a place called Il Roccaforte—and an Italian place, to boot. Rich Italian food two nights in a row. Kerry was going to love that almost as much as renewing her acquaintance with the Footwear Queen herself.

Eberhardt had remembered to switch on the answering machine. But he might as well not have bothered: one hang-up call, followed by the usual screeching mechanical noise that sounds as if somebody is strangling a duck. A wrong number, maybe. Or my mysterious lady caller, whoever *she* was.

I sat down and opened the manila envelope. As Eberhardt had noted, there wasn't much to the report—no essentials that hadn't been in the newspaper stories or that I hadn't found out the past two days. Except, possibly, for one item: Harmon Crane had drawn $2,000 out of his savings account on November 6, the month before his death, and nobody seemed to know why. The money hadn't turned up anywhere among his effects, nor was there any record of what he might have done with it. Yankowski speculated that he might have

lost it gambling—Crane had liked to play poker and the horses now and then—and that its loss had only deepened his depression. Nobody could say for sure if Crane *had* done any gambling during that last month of his life.

The police interrogation of Crane's neighbors had turned up nothing of a suspicious nature; no one had been seen entering or leaving the Crane house around the approximate time of death. Not that that had to mean much either way, though, since the house had been in a wooded area and was somewhat secluded from those near it. Likewise the results of a paraffin test—they were still using it back then—administered to determine if Crane *had* fired the shot that killed him: it had proved inconclusive. Which was the reason why police labs around the country had eventually stopped using paraffin tests; they were notoriously unreliable. As for the coroner's report, it confirmed that Crane had died of a single contact gunshot wound to the left temple and that he had been legally intoxicated at the time of death. And the lab technicians had found nothing questionable in Crane's office, no hint that the shooting might have been anything but a suicide.

Both windows had been latched, fine films of dust on their sills hadn't been disturbed, and nobody could have got in or out that way in any case because the office was on the second floor and there was nothing outside either window to hang onto; a ladder was out of the question because down below was a garden, it had rained heavily that afternoon, and there were no indentations or footprints or other marks in the muddy ground.

The office door had definitely been locked from the inside. The key was still in the latch when Yankowski and Adam Porter broke in, a fact corroborated by both men; the door fit tightly into its frame, making it a physical impossibility for anyone to turn the key from outside by means of string or some other device; and even though the bolt-plate had been torn from the jamb by the forced entry, and both it and the bolt had been damaged, neither had been tampered with beforehand. As far as I could see, the only way it could

71

have been murder was through collusion between Yankowski and Porter—a set-piece carefully arranged before the police were called. But the inspector in charge of the investigation, a man named Gates, had ruled that out. From all I had learned at this late date, I agreed with him. Yankowski and Adam Porter had been anything but bosom pals. Besides which, why would *both* of them have wanted Harmon Crane dead badly enough to conspire to kill him? And for another thing, the circumstances of that night were such that Amanda Crane would also have had to be party to such a plot, and that made no sense at all.

Suicide, all right, I thought. Has to be.

I checked through the list of people Gates and his men had interrogated, looking for someone who had known Crane well enough to offer a theory about the nature of his depression. Aside from Yankowski and the Porters, there wasn't anyone. I wrote down the names of a few people, those who, like Dancer, had been in the same profession and/or who might have been occasional drinking companions. But it seemed a dead-end prospect. On the list were the two writers Kiskadon had spoken to and who hadn't been able to enlighten him; and the rest figured to be long gone from San Francisco or dead by now.

I put the report back in the manila envelope, hauled the phone over, and dialed Stephen Porter's number. I wanted to ask him about Crane's first wife, Ellen Corneal; if he knew what might have become of her. I also wanted to ask him his opinion as to why Crane had withdrawn that $2,000 from his savings account. But talking to him again would have to wait: there was no answer. Late afternoons seemed to be a bad time to try to reach him.

I called Bates and Carpenter. Kerry was on another line; I sat there for five minutes, listening to myself on hold, before she came on. I told her where we were going tonight, and what time, and she said, "Italian *again*? I might have known it. I *hate* that woman, I really do."

"Just grin and bear it, okay?"

"If you promise me this is the last time."

"You know I can't promise you that."

"Oh, all right. The last time for a good long while, then. At least that."

"Deal. How's your day been?"

"Shitty. So my evening better not be."

"It won't," I said, and hoped I wasn't lying in my teeth.

We settled on what time I would pick her up, at which point she had another call and had to ring off. "I should be so popular," I said, but she was already gone.

I swiveled around to the typewriter stand and hammered out a brief report for Michael Kiskadon. I intended to go see him later, so I could check through his Johnny Axe novels; but clients like to have written as well as verbal reports. Words more or less neatly typed on agency stationery reassure them that I'm a sober, industrious, and conscientious detective and give them a feeling of security.

When I was done I dialed Kiskadon's number. Lynn Kidkadon answered. I asked for her husband, and she said, "He's sleeping. Who is this?" Her response when I told her came in a much lower voice, almost a whisper, so I could barely hear her: "Oh, good, I'm glad you called. I've been trying to reach you for two days."

"So you're the woman who's called my office several times."

"Yes."

"Why didn't you leave your name?"

"I didn't want you ringing up here and asking for me if Michael answered."

"Why not?"

"Because I don't want him to know I've gotten in touch with you. I think we need to talk."

"What about?"

"Michael and his father. The job he hired you to do. Can we meet somewhere? Right away?"

"Well . . . I was going to ask your husband if I could stop by."

73

"Here? Why?"

"I need to look at his father's novels."

"What on earth for?"

"To find a name. Look, Mrs. Kiskadon—"

"We could meet in the park," she said, "the one across the street. Just for a few minutes, before you see Michael. Please, it's important."

". . . All right. Where in the park?"

"There's a circle with benches around it, straight across the green from our house and along the first path you come to. You can't miss it. How long will you be?"

"Twenty-five minutes or so."

"I'll be waiting," she said.

The wind off the ocean was pretty stiff today, bending the trees in Golden Gate Heights Park and making humming and rattling noises in their foliage. Nobody was out on the green; the only people I saw anywhere were a couple of kids on the playground equipment on the north side. I parked the car where I had yesterday, across from the Kiskadon house, and crossed the lawn with my head down: the wind slapped at my face and made my eyes water.

I found the path with no trouble, and Mrs. Kiskadon a few seconds later. Huddled inside a white alpaca coat, a bright blue scarf over her short hair, she was sitting on one of the benches at the near end of the circle, opposite a big cedar that grew in its center. She looked cold and solemn and worried.

"Thanks for coming," she said as I sat down beside her. Then she shivered and said, "God, that wind is like ice."

"We could go sit in my car."

"No. Michael was still sleeping when I left, but I don't want to take the chance."

"Why should it matter if he sees you talking to me?"

"He'll figure out why, if he does. Then he'll make trouble for me later on."

"Trouble?"

"He yells," she said, "he says things he doesn't mean. Or maybe he does mean them, I don't know. Then he'll ignore me for days, pretend I'm not even there."

"I don't understand, Mrs. Kiskadon."

"It's his illness," she said. "And his obsession with finding out about his father."

"Suppose you start with the illness."

"Did he tell you what it was? That he almost died from it?"

"He did, yes. Diabetes."

"But I'll bet he didn't tell you what it did to him psychologically. I'm not even sure *he* knows. He used to be optimistic, cheerful . . . normal. Now he has severe mood swings, periods of deep depression. His whole personality has changed."

"That's understandable, given the circumstances."

"That's what his doctor says too. But the doctor doesn't have to live with Michael and I do. He can be . . . well, almost unbearable at times."

"He doesn't get violent, does he?"

"No, no, not toward me. But his depression gets so bad sometimes I think . . ." She broke off and made a fluttery, frustrated gesture with one gloved hand. "He has a gun," she said.

"Gun?"

"A pistol. He keeps it locked up in his den."

"Has he always had it, this pistol?"

"No. He bought it after he came home from the hospital."

"Why?"

"There were reports of prowlers in the neighborhood, a burglary down on Cragmont. He said the gun was for protection."

"But you don't think so?"

"I don't know what to think."

"Has he ever threatened to use it on himself?"

75

"No. But I don't like the idea of it in the house. You can't blame me, can you?"

I didn't say anything. It wasn't a question I could answer.

"Then, there's this obsession with his father," Mrs. Kiskadon said. "It's just not healthy."

"Why do you say that?"

"Because it isn't. It's all he talks about lately, all that seems to interest him. He spent close to two thousand dollars collecting all of his father's writings, and now he wants to spend God-knows-how-much more on a private investigation. We're not rich, you know. We're not even well off anymore."

I had nothing to say to that either.

She said, "You're not even *getting* anywhere, are you? How could you after all those years?"

"I might be," I said carefully.

"I don't care if you are. What does it matter why Harmon Crane shot himself? It's Michael I care about. It's *me*. Don't think my life hasn't been hell this past year because it has."

"So you want me to quit my investigation."

"Yes. It's foolish and it's only feeding his obsession."

"My quitting wouldn't do any good," I said. "As determined as he is, he'd only hire someone else. Someone not as scrupulous as I am, maybe; someone who'd cost him, and you, a lot more money in the long run."

"I didn't mean to imply that you were dishonest. . . ." She broke off again and stared up at the big cedar, as if she thought insight and sympathy might be hiding among its branches. "I don't know what to do," she said in a small voice.

"Have you tried to get him into counseling?"

"A head doctor? He'd never go."

"But have you tried?"

"I mentioned it once. He threw a fit."

"Then I'm sorry, Mrs. Kiskadon, but that's the only advice I can give you."

"You're going to go right on investigating," she said with some bitterness.

"I have to; I made a commitment to your husband. If he asks me to quit, then I will; but it's got to be him. Meanwhile there's a chance, given enough time, that I'll come up with an answer that will satisfy him."

"How much time?"

"I can't answer that yet."

"More than a week?"

"Probably not."

She gnawed flecks of lipstick off her lower lip; one fleck stuck to her front tooth like a dark red cavity. "I suppose you're right," she said at length. The bitterness was gone; she sounded resigned now.

I said, "Why don't you talk to his doctor? A physician might be able to convince him that counseling is a good idea."

"Yes, I'll do that."

I got up on my feet. "You want me to go over first?"

"Please. I'll come in later; he'll think I've been out for a walk."

I left her sitting there, huddled and feeling sorry for herself, and went back along the path and across the green to Twelfth Avenue. Lynn Kiskadon struck me as a self-centered and self-pitying woman, at least as concerned with her own difficulties as she was with her husband's; but I still felt sorry for her. There was no question that she'd had a rough time of it since Kiskadon's illness was diagnosed, and she had stood by him throughout. It would have been nice to do something for her, something noble like take myself off the job as she'd asked, or refuse payment for services rendered. But I wasn't feeling particularly noble these days. Besides which, I like to eat and to pay my bills.

It took Kiskadon almost a minute to answer the doorbell, but he didn't look as if he'd been asleep. He'd been eating something with mustard on it, if the little yellow blob on his chin was any indication. As soon as he saw me his eyes got

bright with anticipation. He said, squirming a little, "Come in, come in. Have you found out something?"

"Not exactly, Mr. Kiskadon."

"Then why. . . ?"

"I'll explain inside."

He let me in, still eager, and limped with me into the big family room. I told him what I'd been doing since we last talked, and why I was here now, and watched him hang on every word as if I had just brought news of a possible miracle cure for his medical condition.

"You're making progress," he said. "I knew you would, I knew it. I'll check the Axe books, you wait right here."

"I can do it. . . ."

"No, no, I think I know which one it is," and he thumped out on his cane, moving more quickly than he had on my last visit here. When he came back after a couple of minutes he said, "It's the last book he wrote, *Axe and Pains*. I was pretty sure it was. The murderer's name is Bertolucci, Angelo Bertolucci."

He handed me the book and I opened it to the last chapter to check the spelling of the name. Kiskadon watched me, rumpling his already tousled clump of black hair.

I asked him, "Does the name mean anything to you?"

"No, nothing."

"No one you talked to mentioned it?"

"I'm sure I'd remember if they had. Are you going out to Tomales now?"

"Not tonight. Tomorrow morning."

"And then what?"

"That depends on what I find out in Tomales."

He had other questions for me, pointless questions that I answered with more patience than I felt. I wanted to get away from there; it was almost six-thirty, and I was picking Kerry up at seven. But that wasn't the only reason. After my talk with Mrs. Kiskadon, the house and Kiskadon's pathetic eagerness were having a depressing effect on me.

I managed to extricate myself with a promise to call him

tomorrow, as soon as I returned from Tomales. He insisted on shaking my hand at the door; his palm was damp and a little clammy, and I had to resist the impulse to wipe my own on my coat when I let go.

Outside, there was no sign of Mrs. Kiskadon. I wondered if she'd slipped into the house while I was there; I hadn't heard her, if so. Or maybe she was still over on that bench in the park, looking for answers to her problems in the branches of the big cedar tree.

NINE

Dinner that evening was more of a disaster than the previous night's earthquake. And I don't mean that metaphorically.

To begin with, I should have known from its location what Il Roccaforte would be like. San Bruno Avenue is not exactly one of the city's ritzier neighborhoods, adjoining as it does the Southern Freeway interchange and the Hunters Point ghetto. I know a guy who lives in that area and he says it's not bad—blue-collar residential, mostly. But it's one of the last places you'd go looking for *haute cuisine* and an elegant, atmospheric dining experience.

The owners of Il Roccaforte had never heard of either *haute cuisine* or elegance. But the place was definitely atmospheric—in the same way a condemned waterfront pier is atmospheric. And without a doubt eating there was one hell of an experience.

It was in a building all its own, so old and creaky-looking it might have been a survivor of the 1906 earthquake, sandwiched between a laundromat and a country-and-western bar called the Bull's Buns. Kerry said, "My God!" in a horrified

voice as we drove up, and I couldn't tell if she meant Il Roccaforte or the Bull's Buns or both. She didn't have anything else to say. She had been conspicuously silent since I'd picked her up, which was always a storm warning with her: it was plain she'd had a *very* bad day in the advertising business, running ideas up flagpoles and seeing if they saluted, or whatever the current Madison Avenue slang expression was, and that she was in no mood for what awaited us inside Il Roccaforte.

Please, Lord, I thought, let it be an uneventful evening. Not a good one, not even a companionable one—just uneventful.

But He wasn't listening.

We got out of the car and went inside. The motif, if you could call it that, was early Depression: some dusty Chianti bottles on shelves here and there, the corpses of three houseplants of dubious origin, a cracked and discolored painting of a peasant woman stomping grapes, tables with linen cloths on them that had not been white since the Truman Administration, and the smells of grease, garlic, and sour wine. Some people might have called the place funky, but none of that type had discovered it yet. The people like myself who called it a relic and a probable health hazard were the ones who, having taken one good look at it, no doubt stayed away in droves. The only customers at the moment, aside from a waiter who looked as if he might have been stuffed and left there for decoration, were Eberhardt and Wanda, tucked up together at a table in one corner.

"Hi, people," Wanda said when we got over there. She beamed at us from under a pair of false eyelashes as big as daddy longlegs and fluffed her gaudy yellow hair and stuck out her chest the way she does, as if anybody but a blind person could miss seeing it. "Say, that's a real cute dress, Kerry. You didn't get that dress at Macy's, did you?"

"No, I didn't."

"Gee, it looks just like one we had on sale last week in the bargain basement."

Kerry smiled with her teeth, like a wolf smiling at a piece of meat, and sat down. There was a carafe of red wine on the table; she picked it up immediately and poured herself a full glass, which she proceeded to sip in a determined way.

I said something to Eberhardt by way of greeting, but he didn't answer. As usual, all his attention was focused on Wanda's chest. Tonight the chest was encased in a white silk blouse with the top three buttons undone, so that most of it, very white and bulging, was visible to the naked eye. Eberhardt's naked eye was full of gleams and glints; I felt like leaning over and telling him to wipe the drool off his chin.

As soon as we were settled, Wanda set the tone for the evening by telling a pair of jokes. Wanda liked to tell jokes, most of which were dumb and a few of which were in bad taste. Sort of like a female Bob Hope.

Wanda: "What's the definition of foreplay in a Jewish marriage?"

Eberhardt: "I dunno, what?"

Wanda: "Thirty minutes of begging."

Eberhardt broke up. I managed a polite chuckle. Kerry just sat there sipping her wine.

Wanda (giggling): "So what's foreplay in an *Italian* marriage?"

Eberhardt: "I dunno, what?"

Wanda: "Guy nudges his wife and says, 'Hey, you ready?'"

Eberhardt broke up again. I managed a polite smile this time, without the chuckle. Kerry just sat there sipping her wine.

"I hear lots of jokes like that down at Macy's," Wanda said. "I could tell jokes like that all night long."

Kerry rolled her eyes and gnashed her teeth a little. Neither Wanda nor Eberhardt noticed. Wanda was still giggling and he was watching her chest and grinning fatuously.

The waiter finally showed up with some menus. He was an older Italian guy dressed up in a shiny, rumpled tuxedo that looked as if it belonged on a corpse. He had a long, sad,

creased face, ears that had big tufts of hair growing out of them, and a toupee so false and loose-fitting that it invited my attention the way Wanda's chest invited Eberhardt's. Every time the waiter leaned over the table, the hairpiece moved a little like something alive that was clinging evilly to the top of his head. If he had heard Wanda's dumb Jewish and Italian jokes, he gave no indication of it. Nor did he bother to adjust his hair. Either he didn't notice it was so loose or he had a lot more faith in its ability to stay put than I did.

He went away and Wanda told us about her day at Macy's. Then she told us another dumb joke. Then she lit up a Tareyton and blew smoke that made Kerry cough and glare and pour more wine. Eberhardt stared at Wanda's chest, still looking both fatuous and horny. I didn't say much. Kerry didn't say anything at all.

The waiter brought us a loaf of bread. I would have eaten some of it, because I was hungry, but if I'd tried I would have broken every tooth in my mouth. It was so old and so hard you couldn't have cut it with a hatchet, much less a knife. It had gone beyond bread and become a whole new and powerful substance. It ought to have been donated to the Giants for use as a fungo bat.

Wanda told us about one of her ex-husbands, the one who had driven a garbage truck; she had two or three, I'm not sure which. One of the things she told us was a long and involved anecdote about his underwear that had no point and wasn't funny but that she concluded with a shriek of laughter so shrill I thought it might shatter the water glasses.

Nobody else came into the place—fortunately for them.

The waiter again, this time to take our orders. I decided his hairpiece looked even more like a spider than Wanda's false eyelashes—a deformed and wicked spider. I almost said, "I'll have the spider, please." Instead I said, "I'll have the scallopini, please." Eberhardt and Wanda both ordered the veal piccata because Wanda said, "They really know how to do it here, Ebbie, you never tasted veal like this before, believe me."

I believed her.

Kerry said, "I'm not very hungry. I guess I'll just have a small salad."

"What's the matter, honey?" Wanda asked her. "Don't you like Italian food?"

"Yes," Kerry said, "but we ate Italian last night. And I'm just not very hungry."

"You sick or something? Getting your period? Sometimes I don't feel like eating much when I'm getting mine."

Kerry buried her nose in her wineglass and sat there looking at the Chianti bottle on the shelf above Wanda's head, as if she wished there would suddenly be another earthquake.

The waiter brought a tureen of soup. When he leaned over to set it on the table I thought for sure his hair was going to fall into the tureen. It didn't, which was something of a disappointment. I *wanted* that damned thing to fall off. We all have our perverse moments, and under the circumstances I felt I was justified in having one of mine.

Wanda told us about the time she went to Tijuana and saw a bullfight. She told us about the highest game she'd ever bowled, "a two-ten, I had *five* strikes in a row, my God I thought I was going to wet my pants." She told us about the time she got drunk at a party and threw up into the heating register. "The place stank for *weeks* after that," she said. "I mean, you just can't get all that stuff *out* of there."

I tried to eat my soup. Minestrone, the waiter had said, lying through his teeth. Maybe it was just the power of suggestion, but what it tasted like was what Wanda had once upchucked into the heating register.

Still no other damn fools came into the place.

Wanda told us about the time she'd had a varicose vein removed from her leg and how painful it was. Then she told us about the time she'd broken her arm roller-skating and how painful that was. Then she told us about the first time she'd had sex and how painful *that* was. "I didn't start to en-

joy it until my fifth or sixth time. How about you, honey?"
she asked Kerry. "You like it the first time you got poked?"

Kerry said something that sounded like "Nrrr." After
which she said between her teeth, "I don't remember."

"Oh, sure you do. Everybody remembers their first time.
How old were you?"

Silence.

"I was fourteen," Wanda said. "The guy lived across the
street, he was fifteen, we did it under the laundry sink in his
basement—I mean, it had to be down there because his parents were home, you know? Boy, was I scared. Fourteen's
pretty young, I guess, but I was a curious kid. How about
you, Ebbie? How old were you?"

"Eighteen," Eberhardt said, staring at her chest.

She looked at me, but I got spared having to answer by
the reappearance of the waiter and his wicked hair. The thing
had slid down over his left ear and seemed to be hanging onto
the edge of it. Fall, you furry bastard, I thought. Fall! But it
didn't.

What the waiter brought this time was a bowl of spaghetti
in marinara sauce. Or what he *said* was spaghetti in marinara
sauce. The minestrone, which had been made out of three
carrots, half a potato, some stringy celery, and a gallon of
peppered water, had had more consistency and more flavor.
But Wanda ate the spaghetti with gusto and half a pound of
parmesan cheese. So did Eberhardt. I ate one strand and a
tiny bit of the marinara sauce, or whatever the hell the red
stuff was, and decided that was enough of a risk for a man my
age. Kerry finished what was left in the wine carafe and ordered a refill.

Wanda talked about her youth in Watsonville, where her
father had been a grower of artichokes. "We never had much
money," she said, "but we had all the artichokes we could
eat. I ate artichokes until they were coming out my ears. I
can't eat them anymore. Just the smell of one cooking makes
me puke."

The main course arrived just then—perfect timing, I

thought, considering Wanda's last comment—and the bowl of spaghetti in marinara sauce got transferred to a sideboard. I was not sorry to see it go. My scallopini had not been made with veal; it had not been made with any sort of animal that had been either young or alive in years. It was so tough you could have used it to make a baseball glove, also for donation to the Giants, a team that needs all the help it can get.

Wanda thought her veal dish was "scrumptious." Eberhardt thought her chest was scrumptious. Kerry took one look at her salad, pushed it away, and poured another glass of wine from the refilled carafe.

Between bites, Wanda talked about another of her ex-husbands, this one a dock worker who used to knock her around when he got drunk. Eberhardt said gallantly that he'd kill any son of a bitch who ever touched her. She rubbed her chest against his arm and batted her eyelashes at him and said, "Oh, Ebbie, you're such a *man!*" If he'd been on the floor at the time he would have rolled over on his back with his tongue lolling out so she could scratch his belly.

The waiter and his pet spider showed up again to ask if we wanted any dessert. Wanda asked him what they had, and he said, "Apple cobbler and zabaglione. But I wouldn't recommend the zabaglione."

"No? Why not?"

"I just wouldn't recommend it," he said ominously.

"Oh. Well, I'll have the apple cobbler then."

None of the rest of us wanted any apple cobbler and definitely not any zabaglione. The waiter went away. Wanda talked. Eberhardt lusted. I fidgeted. Kerry drank. The waiter came back and put a dish of something in front of Wanda and went away again. Eberhardt took his eyes off Wanda's chest long enough to look at the dish.

"Say," he said, "isn't cobbler supposed to have crust?"

"It's got crust," Wanda said.

"Where?"

"There. See? Right there."

Eberhardt looked. I looked too. What she was pointing

at was a little piece of something floating upside down in a brownish goop, like the corpse of some small creature floating on its back in a bog. Then Wanda, the ghoul, proceeded to eat it.

When she was finished she fired up another Tareyton, covered us all with a haze of smoke, and told us about her sister in Minneapolis who was a hairdresser and who worked with "a bunch of faggots, they even got 'em back *there*." Then she gave us her opinion of homosexuality, which was not very high. "You ask me," she said, "that Anita Bryant had the right idea. There oughta be laws against fruits. I mean, the whole idea of them sticking their things into each other—"

"Wanda," Kerry said.

Wanda looked at her. So did I. It was the first word she'd spoken in twenty minutes.

"Why don't you shut up, Wanda," Kerry said.

Wanda said incredulously, "What?"

"Shut up. You know, put your fat lips together so no sound comes out."

Eberhardt said incredulously, "What?"

"You've got diarrhea of the mouth, Wanda."

I said incredulously, "What?"

Everything stopped for a few seconds, like a freeze frame in a movie. We all sat there staring at Kerry. She was sitting stiff and straight, very calm and self-possessed, but her eyes said she was crocked. I also knew her well enough to understand that she was seething inside. Her kettle, as the saying goes, had finally boiled over.

Wanda made a wounded noise, shuffled around in her chair to break the tableau, and said like a siren going off, "You can't talk to me like that! Ebbie, tell her she can't talk to me like that!"

Eberhardt glowered at Kerry. "What's the idea? What's the matter with you?"

"Nothing's the matter with me. The matter is with your fiancée and her big mouth."

"Listen, I don't like that kind of talk—"

86

"Oh, why don't *you* shut up too, Ebbie."

I tried kicking her under the table, but she squirmed her legs out of the way. "Come on, folks," I said like a cheerful idiot, "why don't we all just relax? Kerry didn't mean what she said. She's just—"

"Fed up," Kerry said, "That's what I'm just. And the hell I didn't mean it. I meant every *word* of it."

Wanda pointed a trembly finger at her. "You never liked me. I knew you never liked me right from the first."

"Bingo," Kerry said.

"Well, I never liked you either. You're nothing but a . . . a . . . cold fish. A *scrawny* cold fish."

Kerry's face took on a mottled hue. "Cold fish?" she said. "Scrawny?" she said.

"That's right—scrawny!"

"I'd rather be scrawny than a top-heavy blimp like you."

"Oh, so I'm a blimp, am I? Well, men like big boobs on a woman, not a couple of fried eggs like you got."

Kerry sat absolutely still for maybe three seconds. Then she scraped back her chair and stood up. The rest of us popped up too, like a bunch of jack-in-the-boxes, but Kerry was already moving by then, out away from the table. My first thought was that she was about to stalk off in a huff, but I should have known better; Kerry isn't the type of woman who stalks off in a huff. When I realized what she was really going to do I yelled her name and lunged at her. Too late.

She caught up the bowl of soggy spaghetti from the sideboard and dumped it over Wanda's head.

Wanda let out a screech that rattled the windows. Then she scrunched up her face and segued into wailing hysterics. A strand of spaghetti slid off her nose like a fat red and white worm, dropped onto one enormous breast, and wriggled down its ski-run length, gathering momentum as it went. Some more strands dangled off her ears and around her neck like so much art-deco jewelry. All that spaghetti and all that dripping sauce and all those tears gave her the look of a comic

foil in an old Marx Brothers movie. I managed, just barely, to repress an insane urge to giggle.

Eberhardt was pawing at her with a napkin and his hands, trying to clean her off; all he succeeded in doing was pushing some of the spaghetti down inside her blouse, which only made her yowl the louder. He murdered Kerry with his eyes. Then he murdered me with his eyes. Then he smeared some more marinara sauce into Wanda's chest.

Kerry seemed sobered and a little awed by what she'd done. She said to me in subdued tones, "I think we'd better go. I'll be out in the car." She caught up her purse and off she went, leaving me there to deal with the wreckage alone.

I dealt with it by fumbling my wallet out, throwing a couple of twenties on the table, and saying stupidly, "I'm sorry, Eb. I'll pay for dinner . . ."

"Take your money," he said, snarling the words, "and shove it up your fat ass."

The waiter had come over and was trying to help clean up the mess. His hair had shifted to the right side of his head and was hanging there at a wickedly jaunty angle. I swear he winked at me just before I fled.

TEN

Eberhardt didn't show up at the office next morning. I hung around waiting for him, fidgeting a little. I had an apology speech all worked out, all about how much I regretted what had happened at Il Roccaforte and how contrite Kerry was. Which was the truth: once she'd sobered up last night, and had absorbed the full impact of what she'd done, she had been pretty hangdog about the whole thing. She had tried to call Eberhardt and Wanda, first at his house and then

at her apartment, but nobody answered at either number. So she was planning to go over to Macy's today on her lunch break and apologize to Wanda personally, and then come here to the office and apologize to Eberhardt personally. She had already apologized to *me* personally. I let her do it, but I wasn't really mad at her. I pretended to be, a little, and I pretended to be shocked by such a public loss of control, but secretly I was kind of pleased about it. I kept having mental images of Wanda standing there bawling, with the marinara sauce dripping onto her chest and the spaghetti crawling over her head, and they weren't unpleasant at all. A product of the same sort of perversity that had made me yearn for the waiter's hair to fall off into the soup, with maybe a pinch of malice added.

Wanda was a twit and she'd *deserved* it, by God.

The only thing I was worried about was Eberhardt's reaction. What he'd said to me before I left might have been just words, flung out in the heat of anger; but on the other hand, he was something of a grudge-holder. The last thing I wanted was an episode like last night's putting a damper on our friendship and a strain on our working relationship. Fat-mouth Wanda's feelings weren't worth that. And neither was what I found myself thinking of as the Great Spaghetti Assault.

So I stayed there in the office, waiting for him, instead of getting an early start for Tomales to follow up on the Angelo Bertolucci lead. Keeping busy wasn't much of a problem at first. I called Stephen Porter's number again, found him in, and had a ten-minute talk with him that didn't enlighten me much. In the first place, he hadn't found the box of Harmon Crane's papers yet, even though he was sure they were around "somewhere." And in the second place, while he knew Crane's first wife had been Ellen Corneal, and that they had been married in Reno—an elopement, he said—in 1932, he didn't know what had happened to her after their divorce; nor had he had any idea she'd been pestering Crane for money not long before his suicide.

"Harmon never mentioned her to me," he said. "It was Adam who told me about her."

"Did your brother know if their divorce was amicable or not?"

"He seemed to think it wasn't. One of those brief, youthful marriages that end unhappily when all the passion is spent. I gathered they didn't get on well at all."

"Do you know if she had a profession?"

He paused to think, or maybe just to catch his breath; his coughing and wheezing sounded severe this morning. "No, I can't recall Adam mentioning it, if she did."

"Would you have any idea what she studied at UC?"

"No. You might be able to find that out through the registrar's office, though."

"Might be worth a try. Did you know Russell Dancer?"

"I don't believe I ever met him. The name isn't familiar. You say he knew Harmon fairly well?"

"They were drinking companions for a while."

"Yes, well, people tell each other things when they've been drinking that they wouldn't discuss sober. Or so I'm told. I wish I was a drinking man; I might have got to know Harmon much better than I did. But I haven't much tolerance for alcohol. Two glasses of wine make me light-headed."

"You're probably lucky," I said, thinking of Kerry last night.

When I hung up I dragged the San Francisco telephone directory out of the desk and just for the hell of it looked up Ellen Corneal's name. No listing. I checked my copy of the directory of city addresses, just in case she had an unlisted number. Nothing. So then I called information for the various Bay Area counties; but if Ellen Corneal was still alive and still living in this area, she didn't have a listed phone under that name. Which left me with the Department of Motor Vehicles, a TRW credit check, and the obit file at the *Chronicle*. I put in calls to Harry Fletcher at the DMV, Tom Winters, who was part owner of a leasing company and who had pulled TRWs for me before, and Joe DeFalco at the newspaper office—all

of whom promised to get back to me before the day was out. I decided to forgo a check with the registrar's office at UC until I saw what turned up on the other fronts. Likewise a research trip to the Bureau of Vital Statistics, on the possibility that Ellen Corneal might have remarried here in the city.

Ten-fifteen by this time and still no Eberhardt.

I called his house in Noe Valley. No answer. I went over to his desk and looked up Wanda's home number in his Rolodex and called that. No answer. I called Macy's downtown, and was told that Ms. Jaworski was out ill today.

Well, hell, I thought.

I waited until ten-thirty. Then I scribbled a note that said, *I'm sorry about last night, Eb—we'll talk,* put it on his desk, and left for Tomales. A long drive in the country was just what I needed to soothe my twitchy nerves.

Tomales is a village of maybe two hundred people, clustered among some low foothills along the two-lane Shoreline Highway, sixty miles or so north of San Francisco. But there isn't any shoreline in the immediate vicinity: the village is situated above Tomales Bay and a few miles inland from the ocean. Sheep and dairy ranches surround it, and out where the bay merges with the Pacific there is Dillon Beach and a bunch of summer cottages and new retirement homes called Lawson's Landing. The town itself has a post office, a school, a service station, a general store, a café, the William Tell House restaurant, a church, a graveyard, and thirty or forty scattered houses.

It was well past noon when I got there. The sun was shining, which is something of an uncommon event in the Tomales Bay area, but there was a strong, blustery wind off the ocean that kept the day from being warm. There hadn't been much traffic on the road out from Petaluma, and there wasn't much in Tomales either. What little activity there was in the place was pretty much confined to weekends.

The general store seemed the best place to ask my questions about Angelo Bertolucci; I pulled up in front and went

inside. It was an old country store, the kind you don't see much anymore. Uneven wood floor, long rows of tightly packed shelves, even a big wheel of cheddar cheese on the counter. There weren't any pickle or cracker barrels and there wasn't any pot-bellied stove, but they were about all that was missing. With its smells of old wood, old groceries, fresh bread, and deli meats, the place gave me a faint pang of nostalgia for my long-vanished youth.

Behind the counter was a dark-haired girl of about twenty; she was the only other person in the store. I spent a quarter on a package of Dentyne, and asked her if she lived in Tomales. She said she did. So I asked her if she knew anyone locally named Bertolucci.

"Oh sure," she said. "Old Mr. Bertolucci."

"Old? He's lived here a long time, then?"

"All his life, I guess."

"Would his first name be Angelo?"

"That's right. Do you know him?"

"No. I'd like to talk to him about a business matter."

"Oh," she said, "you want something stuffed."

"Stuffed?"

"A deer or something."

"I don't . . . you mean he's a taxidermist?"

"Didn't you know? He's got all kinds of animals and birds and things in his house. I was there once to deliver groceries when my dad had the flu." A mock shiver. "Creepy," she said.

"How do you mean?"

"All those poor dead things with their eyes looking at you. And Mr. Bertolucci . . . well, if you've ever met him . . ."

"No, I haven't."

"You'll see when you do."

"Is he creepy too?"

"He's kind of, you know—" and she tapped one temple with the tip of her forefinger. "My mother says he's been like that for years. 'Tetched,' she says."

"How old is he?"

"I don't know, seventy or more."

"In what way is he tetched?"

"He hardly ever leaves his house. Everything he wants he has delivered. He's always shooting off his shotgun too. Some kids got in his yard once and he came out with it and threatened to shoot *them*."

"Maybe he just likes his privacy," I said.

"Sure," she said dubiously, "if you say so."

I asked her where Bertolucci lived, and she said on Hill Street and told me the number and how to get there: it was all of three blocks away, off Dillon Beach Road. I thanked her, went out, got into my car, and drove to Hill Street. Some street. An unpaved, rutted dead-end scarcely a block long, with four houses flanking it at wide intervals, two on each side. The first one I passed had a Confederate flag acting as a curtain over its front window; the second one, opposite—a sagging, once-white 1920s frame—was half-hidden by a wild tangle of lilac shrubs and climbing primroses. The second one belonged to Bertolucci.

An unpainted stake fence enclosed the yard; I bumped along and parked in front of its gate. On the gate was a warped sign that said TAXIDERMY in dull black letters. I put a hand against the sign, shoved the gate open, and went along an overgrown path to the porch. Another sign hanging from a nail on the front door invited, *Ring Bell and Come In*. I followed instructions.

The girl at the general store hadn't been exaggerating: the room I walked into was definitely creepy. For one thing it was dim and full of shadows; all the curtains were drawn and the only illumination came from a floor lamp in one corner. There was just enough light so the dozens of glass eyes arranged throughout caught and reflected it in faint, dark glints that made them seem alive. Half a dozen deer heads, one sporting an impressive set of six-point antlers. An elk's head mounted on a massive wooden shield. A game fish of some sort on another shield. On one table, a fat raccoon sitting up

on its hind paws, holding an oyster shell between its forepaws. On another table, an owl with its wings spread and its taloned claws hooked around the remains of a rabbit. Dusty glass display cases bulging with rodents—squirrels, chipmunks, something that might have been a packrat. Two chicken hawks mounted on pedestals, wings half-unfolded and beaks open, glinty eyes staring malevolently at each other, as if they were about to fly into bloody combat. All of that, and a farrago of ancient furniture and just plain junk thrown about in no order whatsoever so that the effect of the place—and the smell that went with it—was of somebody's musty, disused attic.

I was standing there taking it all in when the old man came through a doorway at the rear. He was slat-thin and so stoop-shouldered he seemed to be walking at a low, forward tilt. Thick, knob-knuckled hands, a puff of fuzzy, reddish gray hair like dyed cotton, a nose that resembled the beaks of the two chicken hawks. Dressed in a pair of faded overalls and a tattered gray sweater worn through at both elbows. He was a perfect fit with the rest of the place: old, dusty, frail, and riddled with slow decay.

Or so it seemed until he spoke. When he said, "Yes?" his voice spoiled the impression. It was strong, clear, and more irascible than friendly.

"Mr. Bertolucci?"

"That's right. Help you with something?"

"Possibly. I'd like to—"

"Don't do deer anymore," he said. "Nor elk nor moose nor anything else big. Too much work, too much trouble."

"I'm not here about—"

"Birds," he said, "that's my specialty. Hawks, owls—predators. Nobody does 'em better. Never have, never will."

"I'm not here to have something stuffed and mounted, Mr. Bertolucci. I'd like to ask you a few questions."

"Questions?" He moved closer to me in that crabbed way of his and peered up at my face. His own was swarthy and heavily creased; the lines bracketing his mouth were so deep they looked like incisions that had not yet begun to

bleed. His rheumy old eyes were full of suspicion now, as glass-glinty as those of the stuffed animals and birds. "What questions?"

"About a man named Harmon Crane, a writer who died back in 1949. I wonder if you knew him."

Silence for a time—a long enough time so that it seemed he might not answer at all. His gaze remained fixed on my face. There was a slight puckering of his mouth around badly fitting dentures; otherwise he was expressionless.

"How come?" he said finally.

"How come what, Mr. Bertolucci?"

"How come you're interested in Harmon Crane?"

"You did know him, then?"

"I knew him. Been dead a hell of a long time."

"Yes sir. I'm trying to find out why he killed himself."

"What for, after all these years?"

I explained about Michael Kiskadon. Bertolucci listened with the same lack of expression; when I was done he swung around without speaking, went over to the table with the owl on it, and began to stroke the thing's feathers as if it were alive and a pet. "Ask your questions," he said.

"Did you know Crane well?"

"Well enough not to like him."

"Why is that?"

"Stuck-up. Big-city writer, always tellin people what to do and how to do it. Thought we was all hicks up here."

"You did get along with him, though?"

"We was civil to each other."

"Did you know he used your name in one of his books?"

"Heard it. Didn't like it much."

"But you didn't do anything about it."

"Like what? Sue him? Lawyers cost money."

"You rented Crane a cabin, is that right?"

"Stupidest thing I ever done," he said.

"Why do you say that?"

"Told you. I didn't like him."

"Where was this cabin?"

95

"Not far. Five miles, maybe," Bertolucci said. Slowly, as if he were reluctant to let go of either the words or the information. "End of the big peninsula south of Nick's Cove."

"The cabin still there?"

"Long gone."

"Do you still own the property?"

"No. Sold it to an oyster company in '53, but they went out of business. Man named Corda bought it twenty years ago. Dairy rancher. Still owns it."

The smell in there was beginning to get to me—a musty, gamey mixture of dust, fog-damp, old cooking odors, and the carcasses of all the dead things strewn around. Even breathing through my mouth didn't quite block it out. Another fifteen minutes in there and I'd be ready for stuffing myself.

I asked him, "Do you remember the last time Crane was up here, about six weeks before his suicide?"

Bertolucci gave me a sidewise look. "Why?"

"There was an earthquake while he was here. About as strong as the one the other night."

He didn't say anything at all this time. Just stood there looking at me, still stroking the owl.

"You did see him then, didn't you?"

"No," Bertolucci said.

"Why not?"

"Only time I ever saw him was when he come to town to pay me his rent."

"Then you don't know if anything happened while he was staying at the cabin that last time."

"Happened? What's that mean?"

"Just what I said. Something that depressed him, started him brooding and drinking too much when he went back to San Francisco."

Silence.

I said, "Do you have *any* idea why he killed himself, Mr. Bertolucci?"

More silence. He turned away from the owl, gave me one

96

more expressionless look, and shuffled through the doorway at the rear—gone, just like that.

"Mr. Bertolucci?"

No answer.

I called his name again, and this time a door slammed somewhere at the rear. Ten seconds after that, as I was on my way out, there was a booming explosion from the yard outside, the unmistakable hollow thunder of a shotgun. I reversed direction, shoved through the litter of stuffed animals and furniture, and hauled back the blind that covered one of the side-wall windows. Bertolucci was thirty feet from the house, stooped over in a meager vegetable patch, a big .12-gauge tucked under one arm. When he straightened I saw what he had in his other hand: the bloody, mangled remains of a crow.

I walked to the front door and out to my car. Through the windshield I could see him still standing back there, shotgun in one hand and the dead crow in the other, peering my way.

The girl at the general store hadn't exaggerated him either, I thought. Angelo Bertolucci was every damn bit as creepy as his surroundings.

ELEVEN

I drove south on Shoreline Highway, following the eastern rim of Tomales Bay. The bay is some sixteen miles long and maybe a mile at its widest, sheltered from the rough Pacific storms by a spine of foothills called Inverness Ridge that rises above the western shore. The village of Inverness lies over there, along the water and spreading up into the hills;

and beyond the ridge are the white-chalk cliffs, barren cattle graze, and wind-battered beaches of the Point Reyes National Seashore. On this side are a sprinkling of dairy ranches and fishermen's cottages, a few oyster beds, a boatworks, a couple of seafood restaurants, the tiny hamlet of Marshall, and not much else except more wooded hills and copses of eucalyptus planted as windbreaks. It's a pretty area, rustic, essentially untarnished by the whims of man—one of the last sections of unspoiled country within easy driving distance of San Francisco. That *wouldn't* be the case if it weren't for the weather; developers would have bought up huge chunks of prime bay-front property years ago and built tracts and retirement communities and ersatz-quaint villages, the way they had farther up the coast at Bodega Bay. But down here the fog lingers for days on end, so that everything seems shrouded in a misty, chilly gray. Even on those rare days like this one when the sun shines, the sea wind is almost always blustery and cold; right now, gusting across the bay, it had built whitecaps like rows of lace ruffles on the water, was tossing anchored fishing boats around as if they were toys, and now and then smacked the car hard enough to make it reel a little on the turns. Out on the National Seashore, I thought, it would be blowing up a small gale.

Bad weather doesn't bother me much, though; I come out to Tomales Bay now and then for a picnic, a visit to the Point Reyes lighthouse, fried oysters at Nick's Cove or one of the other seafood restaurants. The bad weather hadn't bothered Harmon Crane, either. It didn't bother the people who lived out here now, nor would it bother the people living elsewhere who could be induced to move here when one or another gambling developer finally pulled the right strings and the inevitable rape of Tomales Bay began. Onward and upward in the name of progress, good old screw-'em-all free enterprise, and the almighty dollar.

Bleak thoughts, a product of the mood Eberhardt's no-show and my unorthodox meeting with Angelo Bertolucci had put me in. Gloom and doom. It was too bad the sun was out;

a dripping gray pall of fog would have been just the right backdrop for a nice, extended mope.

When I passed Nick's Cove I began looking for the peninsula Bertolucci had mentioned. It came up a mile or so farther on: a wide, humpbacked strip of grassland, dotted with scrub oak, that extended out some two hundred yards into the bay. A dirt road snaked up onto it off the highway, vanishing over the crest of the hump; but there was a gate across the road a short ways in and a barbed-wire fence stretching away on both sides. Bushes and a morass of high grass and tall anise blocked my view of the terrain beyond the rise.

Not far away, on the inland side of the highway, was a cluster of ranch buildings surrounded by hilly pastures full of dairy cattle. I drove that way. A lane lined with eucalyptus connected the ranch buildings with the county road, and a sign on one gatepost said CORDA DAIRY RANCH—CLOVER BRAND. I turned into the tunnel formed by the trees, which led me to an old gabled house ringed by bright pink iceplant. A couple of hounds came rushing toward the car, but their tails were in motion and their barks had a welcoming note. One of them jumped up and tried to lick my face when I got out, and a woman's voice called sharply, "Dickens! Down, you! Get down!" She had come out through the front door of the house and was starting toward me. The dog obeyed her, allowing me to go and meet her halfway.

She was in her mid-fifties, pleasant-featured and graying—Mrs. Corda, she said. I showed her the photostat of my investigator's license and told her what I was doing here. Then I asked her if she'd known Harmon Crane.

"No, I'm sorry," she said. "My husband and I are both from Petaluma. We bought this ranch in 1963."

"You do know there was once a cabin out on that peninsula?"

"Yes, but there's almost nothing left of it now. Nor of the oyster company that owned the land before us."

"Would you mind if I had a look around anyway?"

"Whatever for?"

I wasn't sure myself. If I had been a mystic I might have felt I could establish some sort of psychic connection by standing on the same ground Harmon Crane had stood on thirty-five years ago. But I wasn't a mystic. Hell, chalk it up to the fact that I was nosy. It also gave me something to do, now that I was here.

"*Do* you mind, Mrs. Corda?"

"Well, I don't know," she said. "The earthquake the other night opened up some cracks out there. It might be dangerous."

"I'll be careful."

She considered, and I could see her thinking, the way people do nowadays: What if he falls into one of the cracks and breaks a leg or something? What if he sues us? "I don't know," she said again. "You'd better ask my husband."

"Is he here now?"

"No, as a matter of fact he's over on that section. Mending fence that the quake knocked down. He had to take thirty head of cattle off there yesterday."

I thanked her, took the car back out to the highway and up to the dirt road, and turned it along there, stopping nose up to the gate. The wind almost knocked me over when I got out. The gate wasn't locked; I swung it aside and trudged up the incline, bent forward against the force of the wind, the smells of salt water and tideflats sharp in my nostrils. Ahead on my left as I neared the crest I could see the first of the fissures that the earthquake had opened up—a narrow wound maybe three inches wide and several feet long.

From atop the hump I had a clear look at the rest of the peninsula spread out below, sloping downward to the water's edge. A sea of grass and wild mustard, rippling and swaying in odd restless patterns, with one gnarled oak flourishing in the middle of it all like a satisfied hermit. More fissures showed dark brown among the green, half a dozen of them, one at least a foot wide in places, another some fifty feet long. They made me think of the old apocryphal tales of a tremored earth yawning wide and swallowing people, houses, entire

towns. They made me wonder if maybe those tales weren't so apocryphal after all.

There were some other things to see from up there: a newish Ford pickup parked on the road below, and two men off to one side of it, working with hammer and nails, wire and timber, and a post-hole digger to repair a toppled section of fence. They hadn't noticed me yet, and didn't until I got down near the pickup and hailed them. Then they stopped working and watched me warily as I approached.

One of the men was about the same age as the woman down at the ranch—lean, balding, with the kind of face that looks as if somebody had been working on it with an etching tool. The other was more of the same, only at half the age and with all of his hair. Father and son, I thought. Which proved to be the case: the first generation was Emil Corda and the second generation was Gene Corda.

They were friendly enough when I finished showing them my license and telling them what it was I wanted. Emil was, anyway; his son was the taciturn sort and didn't seem overly bright. Emil, in fact, seemed downright pleased with me, as if he welcomed a break in the drudgery of fence-mending. Or as if meeting a private detective who wanted to poke around on his land made this something of a red-letter day for him.

"Guess I don't have any objections to you having a look," he said. "But I'll come along, if it's all the same to you."

"Fine."

"All those cracks—you see 'em out there. Got to watch your step."

I nodded. "Some quake, wasn't it?"

"Yeah it was. Gave us a hell of a scare."

"Me too."

"Next time we get a big one, this whole section's liable to break right off and float on over to Waikiki Beach," he said, and then grinned to show me he was kidding. "Fellow down at Olema claims one of his heifers disappeared into a crack, didn't leave a trace. You believe that?"

101

"Do you?"

"No sir," Corda said. "I've seen cows break a leg in one, I've seen 'em get stuck in one. But swallowed up? Publicity stunt, that's all. Fellow wanted to get his name in the papers." He sounded disappointed as well as disapproving, as if he wished he'd thought of it himself so he would have gotten *his* name in the papers.

I said, "Will you show me where the cabin used to stand, Mr. Corda?"

"Sure thing." He looked at his son. "Gene, you dig another half dozen holes. When I come back we'll anchor those new posts."

The younger Corda mumbled something agreeable, and Emil and I set off toward the far end of the peninsula. The road wasn't much along here, just a couple of grassy ruts, and long before we neared the water it petered out into a cow track. One of the fissures cut a jagged line across it in one place, disappearing into a cluster of poppies.

The outer rim of the peninsula was maybe a hundred feet wide, squared off, with a thin strip of pebbled beach and a couple of acres of mudflats beyond, visible now that the tide was out. The flats weren't being used as oyster beds anymore; at least there was no sign of the poles that are used to fence off most beds. All that was out there was a dozen or so pilings, canted up out of the mud at oblique angles, like a bunch of rotting teeth. I asked Corda about them.

"Oyster company dock," he said. "Big storm broke it up fifteen, sixteen years ago. We managed to salvage some of the lumber."

"Was there also a pier that went with the cabin?"

"Not so far as I know." He gestured to the north, beyond a fan of decaying oyster shells that was half-obliterated by grass. "Cabin was over that way. You can still see part of the foundation."

We went in that direction, up into a little hollow where the remains of a stone foundation rose out of more thick grass

and wild mustard. There wasn't anything else in the hollow, not even a scrap of driftwood.

"What happened to the cabin?" I asked.

"Burned down, so I heard."

"Accident?"

He shrugged. "Couldn't tell you."

"Do you know when it happened?"

"Long time ago. Before the oyster outfit bought the land."

I nodded and moved back to stand on the little strip of beach. Two-thirds of the distance across the bay was an island a few hundred yards in circumference, thickly wooded, with a baby islet alongside it. On the larger island, visible from where I stood now, were the remains of a building—somebody's once-substantial house. Those remains had been there a long time and had always fascinated me. Who would live on a little island in the middle of a fogbound bay?

Not for the first time, I wondered if *I* could do it. Well, maybe. For a while, anyhow. Buy an island like that, build a house on it, wrap myself in solitude and peace. Never mind the wind and fog; all you'd need when the fog rolled in was a hot fire, a good book, and a wicked woman. For that matter, throw in some beer and food and you had all you needed on *any* kind of day.

A seagull came swooping down over the tideflats, screeching the way gulls do. The only other sound was the humming of the wind, punctuated now and then by little wails and moans as it gusted. It had begun to chill me; I could feel goosebumps along my arms and across my shoulders. But I was reluctant to leave just yet. There was something about this place, a sense of isolation that wasn't at all unpleasant. I could understand why Harmon Crane had come here to be by himself. I could understand why he found it a place that stirred his creative juices.

When I turned after a minute or two I saw that Emil Corda had wandered off to the south, following one of the

bigger earth fissures through the rippling grass. I walked over to the fan of oyster shells. As I neared them my foot snagged on something hidden in the grass; I squatted and probed around and came up with part of an old wooden sign, its lettering element-erased to the point where I had to squint at it close up to make out the words: EAST SHORE OYSTER COMPANY. Oddly, it made me think of a marker at a forgotten gravesite.

I straightened, and the wind gusted again and made me shiver, and from forty or fifty yards away Emil Corda let out a shout. I swung around, saw him beckoning to me, and hurried over to where he was, watching my step as I went. He was standing alongside the fissure he'd been following at a place where it was close to a foot wide. There was an odd look on his seamed face, a mixture of puzzlement, awe, and excitement.

"Found something," he said, as if he still didn't quite believe it. "First time I been down this far since the quake."

"Found what?"

"Look for yourself. Down in the crack. This beats that Olema fellow's cow story all to hell. Man, I guess it does!"

I moved over alongside him and bent to peer into the crack. The hairs went up on the back of my neck; a little puzzlement and excitement kindled in me too. Along with a feeling of dark things moving, shifting, building tremors of violence under the surface of what until now had been a routine investigation.

Down at the bottom of that crack were bones, a jumble of old gray bones. The remains of a human skeleton, complete with grinning skull.

TWELVE

Emil Corda and his son drove back to their ranch to call the county sheriff's office. I sat in my car, off to one side of the dirt road, and brooded a little. Those bones out there didn't have to have anything to do with Harmon Crane; they didn't have to be related to his severe depression during those last few months of 1949 and to his eventual suicide. But they were *old* bones, there was no mistake about that. And they looked about the way bones would look if they had lain buried beneath the earth for more than three decades.

No, they didn't have to have anything to do with Harmon Crane. But they did. I knew that, sitting there, as surely as I knew that this was a bad day in October. I felt it in *my* bones.

Corda came back pretty soon, without his son, and I went over and sat in his pickup and talked some. The way he figured it, only the top layers of that fissure were newly split ground; the bottom layers were an old seam, the product of another quake many years ago, that had been gradually sutured and healed and hidden by nature. However the bones had gotten into the original crack, it must have happened while the fissure was still fresh, not too long after the quake that had caused it.

Yeah, I thought. Thirty-five years ago, the quake of October 1949. And maybe it wasn't only nature that had sutured and hid the part of it containing the bones.

A couple of deputy sheriffs arrived within a half hour, and we took them out and showed them what we'd found. One of them got down on his belly, poked around a little, and said, "Some other stuff down here."

"What stuff?" the second deputy asked.

"Dunno yet. Something that looks like . . . hell, I don't know, a cigarette case, maybe. Few other things too. It's all pretty dirty and corroded."

"Better leave it be until San Rafael gets here."

The one deputy got up and we all trooped back out by the highway, playing question-and-answer on the way. I told the deputies why I was there and let them draw their own conclusions, not that either of them seemed particularly interested. Old bones didn't excite them much. New bones, on the other hand, would probably have had them in a dither.

It was another twenty minutes before "San Rafael"—a reference to the Marin county seat—arrived in the person of a plainclothes investigator named Chet DeKalb and a technician with a portable field kit. We went through the same routine of going out to look at the bones, of Corda and me explaining how we'd found them and what my business there was. DeKalb seemed a little more interested than the two deputies, but not much. He was in his forties, thin and houndish, with a face that looked as if it would crack wide open if he ever decided to smile. He was the unflappable type. A room full of corpses might have thrilled him a little; bones, old or new, didn't even raise an eyebrow.

He and the lab guy began to fish out the bones and bone fragments and other objects from the fissure, with the technician bagging and labeling them. The rest of us stood around and watched and shivered in the icy wind. I moved up for a look at the other items as they came out; as near as I could tell, they included a cigarette case or large woman's compact, some keys, a lump of something that might have been jewelry—a brooch, maybe—and a couple of rusted things that appeared to be buckles. I also took a close look at the skull when DeKalb handed it up to the lab man. It was badly crushed in a couple of places, probably as a result of its internment in the fissure. It would take a forensic expert to determine if any damage had been done to the skull or any of the other bones prior to burial.

When he was satisfied they'd got everything out of the crack, DeKalb led the parade back to where the cars were parked. He took down my address and telephone number, asked a few more questions about Harmon Crane, and said he might want to talk to me again later on. Then he and the

technician went away with the bones and other stuff, and the two deputies disappeared, and Corda said he'd better get back home, his wife and son were waiting and besides, it wasn't every day somebody found a bunch of human bones on his property and maybe a reporter from one of the newspapers would want to contact him about it. From the look in his eyes, if a reporter *didn't* contact him pretty soon he'd go ahead and contact a reporter.

Before long I was standing there alone, shivering in the wind and watching sunset colors seep into the sky above Inverness Ridge. For no reason I walked up on top of the hump again and looked out over the peninsula, out over the bay to the wooded island, its ruins dark now with the first shadows of twilight.

Maybe I wouldn't want to live out there after all, I thought. Or maybe it's just that I wouldn't want to die out there, all alone in the cold and the fog and that endless wind.

Six o'clock had come and gone when I got back to San Francisco. I went to the office first, found it still locked up as I'd left it. Eberhardt hadn't come in; the note I'd written him was right where I had put it on his desk blotter. I checked the answering machine: three calls, all from the contacts I had phoned earlier and all negative. No one named Ellen Corneal had died in San Francisco during the past thirty-five years; but neither was anyone named Ellen Corneal registered with the DMV, or the owner of any of the dozens of available credit cards.

For a time I stood looking at my phone, thinking that I ought to call Michael Kiskadon. But I didn't do it. What could I tell him? Maybe his father had perpetrated or been involved in some sort of criminal activity and maybe he hadn't been; maybe those bones were why he'd shot himself and maybe they weren't. Not enough facts yet. And Kiskadon had too many problems as it was without compounding them for no good reason.

The office, after Eberhardt's continued absence, and with

darkness pressing at the windows, only added to the funk I was in. I shut off the lights, locked the door again, and went away from there.

Kerry said, "Where can he be, for God's sake? I must have tried calling him half a dozen times today and tonight."

She was talking about Eberhardt, of course. We were sitting in the front room of my flat; she had been waiting for me there, working on a glass of wine and her own funk, rereading one of her mother's Samuel Leatherman stories in an old issue of *Midnight Detective*. She did that sometimes—came by on her own initiative, to wait for me. We practically shared the place anyway, just as we shared her apartment on Diamond Heights. She had put a roast in the oven and the smell of it was making my mouth water and my stomach rumble. I drank some more of my beer to quiet the inner man until the roast could do the job right and proper.

"I called Wanda too," Kerry said. "Somebody at Macy's told me she was home sick, but she hasn't answered her phone all day. The two of them must have gone off somewhere together."

"Probably."

"But where? Where would they go?"

"The mountains, up or down the coast—who knows?"

"Just because of what I did to Wanda?"

I shrugged. "Maybe they decided to elope."

She looked at me over the rim of her wineglass. I had said it as a joke, but she wasn't laughing. For that matter, neither was I.

"You really think they'd do that?" she asked.

"No," I lied.

"God, I can't imagine Eberhardt married to that woman."

"Neither can I. I don't even want to try. Let's talk about something else. That roast out there, for instance."

"Ten more minutes. Tell me some more about the bones you found."

"There's nothing more to tell. All I know right now is that they're human. And *I* didn't find them; Emil Corda did."

"Well, he wouldn't have if you hadn't been there," she said. "What are the chances the Marin authorities can identify them?"

"Hard to say. Modern technology isn't infallible."

"Can't they do it through dental charts and things like that?"

"Maybe. It all depends."

"On what?"

"On how long ago the victim was buried. On how much dental work he or she had done. On whether or not the dentist is still alive and can be found. On a whole lot of other factors."

"Victim," Kerry said. "Uh-huh."

"What?"

"You used the word *victim*. You think it was murder, don't you."

"Not necessarily."

"It *has* to be murder," she said. "People don't bury bodies in convenient earth fissures unless they're trying to cover up a homicide."

"By 'people' I suppose you mean Harmon Crane."

"Who else? He killed some woman up there, that's obvious."

"Is it? Why do you think it was a woman?"

"He had a frigid wife, didn't he? Besides, there's that cigarette case—"

"Men also carried cigarette cases back then, you know."

"—*and* the brooch. Men didn't wear brooches back then."

"If it was a brooch."

"Of course it was. The brooch and the cigarette case and the keys and other items must have been in her purse. He buried the purse with her and it rotted away to nothing, leaving the buckles. Simple."

109

I sighed. Kerry fancies herself a budding detective; and ever since she'd had some success along those lines—as a buttinsky on a case of mine in Shasta County this past spring, at considerable peril to her life and my sanity—she had been slightly insufferable where her supposed deductive abilities were concerned. It was a bone of contention between us, but I didn't feel like worrying it anymore right now. The only bone I wanted to worry tonight was the one in that roast in the oven.

"Go check on dinner, will you?" I said. "I'm starving here."

"You're always starving," she said, but she got up and carried her empty wineglass into the kitchen with her. She was just the slightest bit sloshed again tonight, a state to which she was entitled considering how hard she'd been working and her futile efforts to soothe her conscience about last night's fiasco. Not to mention her ex-husband, Ray Dunston, who had given up his law practice a while back to join a Southern California religious cult and who was pestering her to "re-mate" with him in a new life of communal bliss and daily prayer chants. But if being sloshed again was an omen of things to come, I didn't like it much. I had already had a demonstration of Kerry's impulsive behavior while under the influence, and one demonstration was all I wanted to witness, thank you.

I wandered over to the nearest shelf of my pulps and browsed through a few issues at random. I was in the mood for pulp tonight. *Bad* pulp. Something by Robert Leslie Bellem from *Spicy Detective,* for instance. I found a 1935 issue with two stories by Bellem—one, under a pseudonym, called "The Fall of Frisco Freddie"—and took it back to the couch. But I couldn't concentrate yet. That damned roast . . .

I got up again and lumbered into the kitchen. Kerry had the roast out; but she said, "Five more minutes," and started to push it back into the oven again. I said, "Give me that thing, I don't care if it's done or not," and grabbed a carving

110

knife out of the rack and hacked off an end and stuffed it into my mouth.

Kerry said, "Barbarian."

I said, "Mmmmff."

It was a good roast. It was so good, in fact, that it put an end to my funk, allowed me to enjoy "The Fall of Frisco Freddie" a little while later, and to bring about the Lay of Kerry Wade a little while after that.

The lay kept her from inhaling any more wine, which was my primary intention, of course. The things I do to maintain harmony in my life. . . .

THIRTEEN

On Thursday morning, without stopping at the office, I drove back across the Bay to Berkeley. I was not about to make a habit of hanging around waiting for Eberhardt to get over his mad and come back to work. Or of worrying that he wouldn't do either one. If the Il Roccaforte incident loomed large enough for him to bust up both our friendship and our partnership, then he was a damn fool and there was no use making myself crazy over the fact. I had enough trouble trying to shepherd one damn fool through life—me— without fretting and stewing about another one.

Some mood I was in again this morning. And for no particular reason I could figure out, except that the fog had come in during the night and the day was gray and bleak. Even in normally sunny Berkeley it was gray and bleak, which would make Telegraph Avenue even harder to take than usual.

But the first place I went was to Linden Street, to the house where Amanda Crane lived with her niece. Not to see

Mrs. Crane this time; it was the niece I wanted a conversation with—if I could break through her defenses long enough to get one. She must know the full story of what had happened back in 1949 and she might have picked up something from Mrs. Crane, or from some other source, that would be of help.

Moot possibility for now, though: neither she nor Amanda Crane was home. Or if they were, they weren't answering the doorbell for the likes of me.

I drove downtown via Shattuck, found a place to park on Channing Way, walked back to Telegraph, and turned north toward the Bancroft gate to the UC campus. The sidewalks were crowded with the usual admixture of students, shoppers, hustlers, dope peddlers and buyers, musicians, street artists selling everything from cheap jewelry to hand-carved hash pipes, and assorted misfits. A girl wearing a poncho and half a pound of brass bracelets, rings, earrings, and neck adornments leaned against an empty storefront and sang Joan Baez protest songs to her own guitar accompaniment; a red-and-white emblem on the base part of the guitar said *Death to the Warmongers*. A young-old paraplegic rumbled past me in a motorized wheelchair, going somewhere in a hurry, or maybe going nowhere at all. You see a lot of paraplegics on the streets of Berkeley—some born that way, others the wasted and forgotten residue of Vietnam. Three different kids tried to panhandle me in the two blocks to Bancroft, one of them stoned on some sort of controlled substance that gave him the vacuous, drooling expression of an idiot. A bag lady dressed in black knelt in the gutter to pry loose a crushed Coca-Cola can that was wedged in a sewer grating. A man carrying a Bible in one hand and a stack of leaflets in the other told me God was angry, God would not contain His wrath much longer, and handed me a leaflet that bore a pair of headlines in bold black type: THE END IS NEAR—BE PREPARED! THERE IS NO ESCAPING JUDGMENT DAY!

Go tell it on a mountain, brother, I thought. Maybe then someone will listen.

The street depressed me; it always did. The ugliness, the pervasive sense of hopelessness. The waste. And we were all to blame—mankind was to blame. We had all created the Telegraph Avenues of this world just as surely as we had created war and nurtured greed and applauded the actions of fools and knaves these past eighty-odd years. Some century, the twentieth. The age of enlightenment, understanding, wisdom, and compassion.

Cynical philosophy on a cold, bleak October morning. Maybe I ought to stand next to the guy with the leaflets, I thought, and shout it out for all to hear. Then passersby could laugh at me too: just another freak in the Telegraph Avenue sideshow.

The UC campus was something of an antidote for the depression, at least. Clean, attractive, well cared for; crowded with kids who for the most part looked like typical college students. I wandered among them, past the Student Union and Ludwig's Fountain to Sproul Hall. Sproul was where the registrar's office was, on the first floor. Except for a couple of student clerks, there was nobody in it when I entered. The rush for fall registration had long since ended and things were quiet here at this time of year.

The clerk who waited on me was a young woman with a body like a colt and a face like the colt's mother: pointy ears, hair that hung down over her eyes, a long muzzle, and lots of teeth. I told her my name was William Collins and that I was a writer doing a biography about a former Cal student in the thirties, a well-known mystery writer named Harmon Crane. She had never heard of Harmon Crane—she didn't read mysteries, she said snootily; they had no redeeming literary merit; *she* read Proust, Sartre, Joyce.

Proust to Sartre to Joyce, the old double-play combination, I thought in my lowbrow way. But I didn't say it.

I said I was trying to track down information about Harmon Crane's first wife, Ellen Corneal, who had also been a student at UC in the early thirties, and would it be possible for her to let me see Ellen Corneal's records? She said no,

113

absolutely not, it was against school policy. I argued, reasonably enough, that those records were now half a century old and that no harm could possibly be done by me seeing them at this late date. I appealed to her sense of literary history, even though we were only talking about a lowly mystery writer here. I can be persuasive sometimes, and this was one of them: I could see her weakening.

"I can't let you *see* the records," she said. She was firm about that. "Definitely not."

"How about if I ask you some questions and you tell me the answers?"

"I can't answer any questions about a person's admissions materials," she said.

"Then I won't ask any."

"Or about transcripts."

"No questions about those, either."

"Or written evaluations, personal or classroom."

"Just background data, that's all."

She relented finally, said it would take a while to look through the files, and suggested I go away and come back again in an hour. So I went out and walked around the campus, all the way past the Earth Sciences buildings to the North Gate and back again, and was standing in front of the horse-faced clerk in exactly one hour.

"You're very prompt," she said, and showed me some of her teeth. I half expected her to whinny a little to emphasize her approval of punctuality.

I asked her some questions about Ellen Corneal's family background; she kept the records at a safe distance while she consulted them and provided answers, as if she were afraid I might leap over the counter and yank them out of her hands. But what she told me wasn't very helpful. Ellen Corneal had been born in Bemidji, Minnesota; her mother had died when she was two, her father when she was eleven, and she had come to California to live with a maiden aunt after the father's death. She had no siblings and no other relatives. The aunt had been sixty-two-years old in 1932, when Ellen Corneal entered

114

UC, and would now be one hundred and fourteen years old if she were still alive, which was a highly unlikely prospect. The Corneal woman had dropped out of school in 1933, after marrying Harmon Crane, but had returned two years later to finish out her schooling and earn her degree.

"In what?" I asked.

"I beg your pardon?"

"In what did she earn her degree? What was her major?"

"Oh. A B.A. in cartography."

"Map-making?"

"That is what cartography *is*, sir."

"Uh-huh. An unusual profession."

"I suppose you might say that. At least it was for a woman back then."

"Women have come a long way," I said, and smiled at her.

She didn't smile back. "We still have a long way to go," she said. From the ominous note in her voice, she might have been issuing a warning. I wanted to tell her that I wasn't the enemy—Kerry had once called *me* a feminist, in all sincerity, something I still considered a high compliment—but trying to explain myself to a twenty-year-old woman who read Proust and Sartre and Joyce and thought mysteries were trash was an undertaking that would have required weeks, not to mention far more patience than I possessed. I thanked her again instead and left Sproul Hall and then the campus through the Bancroft gate.

But I didn't go back down Telegraph Avenue to get to my car; I took the long way around, up Bancroft and down Bowditch. One trip through the sideshow was all I could stand today.

There was still nobody home on Linden Street. So I drove back across the Bay Bridge, put my car in the garage on O'Farrell, and went up to the office. The door was unlocked; and when I opened it and walked in, there was Eberhardt sitting behind his desk, scowling down at some papers spread

115

out in front of him. He transferred the scowl to me as I shut the door, but he didn't say anything. So I did the ice-breaking myself.

"Well, well," I said. "Look who's here."

"I don't want to talk about it," he said.

"Talk about what?"

"You know what. I'm not talking about it."

"All right."

"Business, that's all. Just business."

"Whatever you say, Eb."

"Kerry called, I told her the same thing."

"What did she say to that?"

"What do you think she said? She said okay."

"Good."

"Yeah. Good. You got two calls this morning."

"From?"

"Michael Kiskadon both times. He wants you to call him."

"He say what he wanted?"

"No. But he sounded pissed." Eberhardt paused and then said, "Kerry do something to him too?"

"I thought you didn't want to talk about that."

"What?"

"What happened at Il Roccaforte."

"I don't. I told you that."

"Okay by me."

I hung up my hat and coat, poured myself a cup of coffee, and sat down at my desk with it. Eberhardt watched me without speaking as I dialed Kiskadon's number.

Kiskadon was angry, all right. He answered on the first ring, as if he'd been hovering around the phone, and as soon as I gave my name he said, "Damn it, why didn't you call me yesterday? Why didn't you tell me what's going on?"

"I'm not sure I know what you mean."

"The hell you don't know what I mean. Those bones you found up at Tomales Bay."

"How did you hear—?"

"The Marin County Sheriff's office, that's how. Sergeant DeKalb. He wanted to verify that you're working for me. *Are* you, or what?"

"Working for you? Of course I am—"

"Then why didn't you call me? How do you think I felt, hearing it from that cop?"

"Look, Mr. Kiskadon," I said with forced patience, "I didn't call you because there wasn't anything definite to report. Those bones may have nothing to do with your father."

"Maybe you believe that but I don't. They're connected with his suicide, they have to be."

I didn't say anything.

"They were a *woman's* bones," Kiskadon said.

"Did Sergeant DeKalb tell you that?"

"Yes. Something he found with the bones confirmed that."

"What something?"

"He wouldn't tell me. Nobody tells me anything." Now he sounded petulant. "I thought I could trust you," he said.

"You can. I told you, I didn't call because—"

"I want to know everything from now on," he said. "Do you understand? Everything you do, everything you find out."

I was silent again.

"Are you still there?"

"I'm still here," I said. "But I won't be much longer if you start handing me ultimatums. I don't do business that way."

Silence from him this time. Then he said, with less heat and more petulance, "I wasn't giving you an ultimatum."

"That's good. And I wasn't withholding anything from you; I don't do business that way either. When I have something concrete to report I'll notify you. Now suppose you let me get on with my work?"

". . . All right. I'm sorry, I didn't mean to blow up at you like that. It's just that . . . those bones, buried up there like that . . . I don't know what to think."

"Don't think anything," I said. "Wait for some more facts. Good-bye for now, Mr. Kiskadon; I'll be in touch."

"Yes," he said, and both the anger and the petulance were gone and that one word was cloaked in gloom.

Manic depressive, I thought as I put the receiver down. His wife was right about him; if she didn't get him some help pretty soon, somebody to fix his head, he was liable to crack up. And then what? What happens to a guy like Kiskadon when he falls over the line?

Eberhardt was still watching me. He said, "What was that all about? That stuff about bones?"

I told him. Then I asked, "Do you know a Marin Sheriff's investigator named DeKalb?"

"What's his first name?"

"Chet."

"Yeah, I know him. Why?"

"I could use an update on those bones and the other stuff from the fissure. I'm not sure he'd give it to me."

"But you think he might give it to me."

"He might. You mind calling him?"

"Shit," he said, but he reached for his phone just the same.

I got out the Yellow Pages and looked up Professional Organizations. No listing for cartographers, not that that was very surprising. So then I looked up the number for the big Rand McNally store downtown, Rand McNally being the largest map company around, and dialed it and asked to speak to somebody who could help me with a question about cartographers. A guy came on after a time, and I asked him if there was a professional organization for map-makers, and he said there was—The American Society of Cartographers—and gave me a local number to call. I also asked him if he knew a cartographer named Ellen Corneal, but he had never heard of her.

When I dialed the number the Rand McNally guy had given me, an old man with a shaky voice answered and said that yes, he was a member of the American Society of Car-

118

tographers and had been for forty-four years; he sounded ancient enough to have been a member for *sixty*-four years. I asked him if he knew a cartographer named Ellen Corneal who had graduated from Cal in 1938.

"Corneal, Corneal," he said. "Name's familiar . . . yes, but I can't quite place it. Hold on a minute, young man."

Young man, I thought, and smiled. The smile made Eberhardt, who was off the phone now and watching me again, scowl all the harder.

The old guy came back on the line. "Yes, yes," he said, "I thought I recognized the name. Ellen Corneal Brown."

"Sir?"

"Her married name. Brown. Her husband is Randolph Brown."

"Also a cartographer?"

"Well, of course. The man is quite well known."

"Yes, sir. Do you know if she's still alive?"

"Eh? Alive? Of course she is. At least, she paid her dues this year."

"Can you tell me where she lives?"

"No, no, can't do that. Privileged information."

"But she does reside in the Bay Area?"

"I'm sorry, young man."

"Would you at least give me a number where I can reach her?"

"Why? What do you want with her?"

I told him I was a writer doing a free-lance article on map-making, emphasis on women cartographers. That satisfied him; he gave me the number. No area code, which made it local. And from the first three numbers, it sounded like a Peninsula location—San Bruno, Millbrae, maybe Burlingame.

Eberhardt said when I hung up, "DeKalb's out somewhere and won't be back until after one. I'll call him back."

"Thanks, Eb."

"Goddamn flunky, that's all I am around here. Take

119

messages, call up people, type reports. Might as well be your frigging secretary."

"You'd look lousy in a dress," I said.

"Funny," he said.

"Who wants a secretary with hairy legs?"

"Hilarious," he said. "See how I'm laughing?"

I dialed Ellen Corneal Brown's number. A woman answered, elderly but not anywhere near as shaky as the society representative, and admitted to being Ellen Corneal Brown. I told her how I'd gotten her number and asked if she was the Ellen Corneal who had graduated from UC in 1938. She said she was. I asked if I might stop by and interview her as part of a project involving her past history—not lying to her but letting her make the assumption that it was her past history in the field of cartography that I was interested in. She wasn't the overly suspicious type, at least not without sufficient cause. She said yes, she supposed she could let me have a few minutes this afternoon, would two o'clock be all right? Two o'clock would be fine, I said, and she gave me an address on Red Ridge Road in the Millbrae hills, and that was all there was to it. It happens that way sometimes. Days when things fall into place without much effort and hardly any snags.

But not very often.

I finished my coffee and got on my feet. "I think I'll go get some lunch," I said to Eberhardt. "You want to join me?"

"No. I'm not hungry."

"Late breakfast?"

"I'm just not hungry. Why don't you go eat with Kerry?"

"She's got a business lunch today."

"Big agency client, huh?"

"Reasonably big."

"Well, I hope she doesn't get drunk and decide to dump a bowl of spaghetti over *his* head."

I didn't respond to that.

"That was a goddamn lousy thing she did the other night, you know that?" he said.

120

"You change your mind, Eb?"

"About what?"

"Talking out what happened at Il Roccaforte?"

"No. You heard me tell you I don't want to talk about it."

"Then why do you *keep* talking about it?"

"*I'm* not talking about it, *you're* talking about it. What the hell's the matter with you, anyway?"

I sighed. Eb, I said, sometimes I think you and Wanda deserve each other. But I said it to myself, not to him. I put my coat and hat on and opened the door.

Behind me Eberhardt muttered, "Tells her to shut her fat mouth and then dumps a goddamn bowl of spaghetti over her head, Jesus Christ!"

I went out and shut the door quietly behind me.

FOURTEEN

Red Ridge Road was a short, winding street shaded by old trees a dozen miles south of San Francisco and a half-mile or so downhill from Highway 280. It hadn't been built on a ridge and if any of the earth in the vicinity had ever been red, there was no longer any indication of it. Score another point for our sly old friends, the developers. A lot of the houses up there had broad, distant views of the Bay; others were half-hidden in copses of trees; still others sat at odd angles, on not much land and without much privacy, like squeezed-in afterthoughts. The house where Ellen Corneal Brown lived was one of the last group—a smallish split-level with a redwood-shake roof and an attached garage, primarily distinguished from its neighbors by a phalanx of camellia bushes that were now in bright red and pink blossom.

121

I parked at the curb in front, ran the camellia gauntlet, and rang the bell. The woman who opened the door was in her seventies, on the hefty side and trying to conceal it inside a loose-fitting dress. White hair worn short and carefully arranged, as if she had just come from the beauty parlor. Sharp, steady eyes and a nose that came to an oblique point at the tip.

I said, "Mrs. Brown?"

"Yes. You're the gentleman who called?"

"Yes, ma'am."

She kept me standing there another five seconds or so, while she looked me over. I looked her over too, but not in the same way. I was trying to imagine what she'd looked like fifty years ago, when she and Harmon Crane had gotten married, and not having any luck. She was one of those elderly people who look as if they were born old, as if they'd sprung from the womb white-haired and age-wrinkled like leprechauns or gnomes. I couldn't even decide if she'd been attractive, back in the days of her youth. She wasn't attractive now, nor was she unattractive. She was just elderly.

I must have passed muster myself because she said, "Come in, please," and allowed me a small cordial smile. "We'll talk in the parlor."

Age hadn't slowed her up much; she got around briskly and without any aids. The room she showed me into was a living room; "parlor" was an affectation. But it wasn't an ordinary living room. If I hadn't known her profession, and that of her husband, one look would have enabled me to figure it out.

The room was full of maps. Framed and unframed on the walls, one hanging suspended from the ceiling on thin gold chains, three in the form of globes set into antique wooden frames. Old maps and new maps. Topographic maps, geological maps, hydrographic and aviation charts. Strange maps I couldn't even begin to guess the purpose of, one of them marked with the words *azimuthal projection*, which for all I

knew charted the geographical distribution of bronchial patients.

Mrs. Brown was watching me expectantly, waiting for a reaction, so I said, "Very impressive collection you have here."

She nodded: that was what she wanted to hear. "My husband's, mostly, acquired before we were married, although I have contributed a few items myself. Some are extremely rare, you know."

"I'm sure they are."

"That gnomonic projection of the Indian Ocean," she said, pointing, "dates back to the 1700s. The hachures are still quite vivid, don't you think?"

Hachures. It sounded like a sneeze. I nodded wisely and kept my mouth shut.

"Sit down, won't you," Mrs. Brown said. "I have coffee or tea, if you'd care for a hot drink."

"Nothing, thanks."

I waited until she lowered her broad beam onto a quilted blue-and-white sofa and then lowered mine onto a matching chair nearby. Mrs. Brown said, "Well then. You're interested in my cartographic work, I believe you said."

"Well . . ."

"My major contribution," she said proudly, a little boastfully, "was in the area of conic projections. I developed a variant using the Lambert conformal conic projection in conjunction with the polyconic projection, so that—"

"Uh, Mrs. Brown, excuse me but I don't understand a word you're saying."

She blinked at me. "Don't understand?"

"No, ma'am. I don't know the first thing about maps."

"But on the telephone . . . you said . . ."

"I said I was interested in talking to you about your past history. I didn't mean your professional history; I meant your personal history. I'm sorry if you got the wrong impression," I lied. "I didn't mean to deceive you."

She sat looking bewildered for a few seconds. Then her eyes got flinty and her jaw got tight and I had a glimpse of another side of Ellen Corneal Brown, a less genteel and pleasant side that hadn't been softened much by the advent of old age.

"Who are you?" she said.

"A private detective. From San Francisco."

"My God. What do you want with me?"

"The answers to a few questions, that's all."

"What questions?"

"About your first husband, Harmon Crane."

The eyes got even flintier; if she hadn't been curious, she would have told me to get the hell out of her house. But she was curious. She said, "Mr. Crane has been dead for more than thirty years."

"Yes, ma'am, I know. I'm trying to find out why he committed suicide."

"Do you expect me to believe that? After all this time?"

"It's the truth."

"Who is your client?"

"His son, Michael Kiskadon."

"Son? Mr. Crane had no children."

"But he did. His second wife bore him a son after they were divorced and kept it a secret from him. He died without ever knowing he was a father."

She thought that over. "Why would the son wait so many years to have Mr. Crane's suicide investigated? Why would he want to in the first place?"

I explained it all to her. She struggled with it at first, but when I offered to give her Kiskadon's address and telephone number, plus a few other references, she came around to a grudging acceptance. I watched another struggle start up then, between her curiosity and a reluctance to talk about either Harmon Crane or her relationship with him. Maybe she had something to hide and maybe it was just that she preferred not to disinter the past. In any case she was what the lawyers call a hostile witness. If I didn't handle her just right

she would keep whatever she knew locked away inside her, under guard, and nobody would ever get it out.

I asked her, "Mrs. Brown, do you have any idea why Crane shot himself?"

"No," she said, tight-lipped.

"None at all? Not even a guess?"

"No."

"Did you have any inkling at the time that he was thinking of taking his own life?"

"Of course not."

"But you did see him not long before his suicide?"

She hesitated. Then, warily, "What makes you think that? We had been divorced for fourteen years in 1949."

"He mentioned to a friend in September or October of that year that you'd been to see him."

"What friend?"

"A writer named Russell Dancer."

"I don't know that name. Perhaps he has a faulty memory."

"Does that mean you *didn't* visit Crane at that time?"

Another hesitation. "I don't remember," she said stiffly.

"Were you living in San Francisco in 1949?"

"No."

"In the Bay Area?"

". . . In Berkeley."

"Working as a cartographer?"

"Yes. I was with *National Geographic* then."

"Married to your present husband?"

"No. Randolph and I were married in 1956."

"You lived alone in Berkeley, then?"

"I did."

"You must have been making a good salary."

"It was . . . adequate. I don't see what—"

"Then you weren't poor at the time," I said. "You didn't need a large sum of money for any reason. Say two thousand dollars."

Her lips thinned out again, until they were like a horizon-

tal line drawn across the lower half of her face. "Did this Dancer person tell you I tried to get money from Mr. Crane?"

"Did you, Mrs. Brown?"

"I won't answer that."

"Did Crane give you two thousand dollars the month before his death?"

No response. She sat there with her hands twisted together in her lap, glaring at me.

"Why did he give you that much money, Mrs. Brown?"

No response.

"Was it a loan?"

No response.

"All right," I said, "we won't talk about the money. Just tell me this: Did you visit Crane at his cabin at Tomales Bay?"

She took that one stoically, but her eyes said she knew what I was talking about. "I don't know what you're talking about," she said.

"Surely you must have known about his little retreat."

"No. How would I know?"

"It was common knowledge he went up there alone to write."

No response.

"*Did* you visit him there, Mrs. Brown?"

She got up on her feet, a little awkwardly because of her bulk and age, and gestured toward the entrance hall. "Get out of my house," she said. "This minute, or I'll call the police."

I stayed where I was. "Why? What are you afraid of?"

"I'm not afraid," she said. "You and I have nothing more to say to each other. And my husband is due home from the country club any time; I don't want you here when he arrives."

"No? Why not?"

"You'll upset him. He has a heart condition."

"Maybe I ought to talk to him just the same."

"You wouldn't dare."

She was right: I wouldn't, not if he had a heart condition. But I said, "He might be more cooperative than you've been," and I felt like a heel for badgering an old lady this way, even an unlikable old lady like Ellen Corneal Brown. But playing the heel is part of the job sometimes. Nobody ever said detective work was a gentleman's game, not even the coke-sniffing master of 221-B Baker Street himself.

"Randolph knows nothing about that part of my life," Mrs. Brown said. She was standing next to one of the antique globes; she reached down and gave it an aggravated spin. "And I don't want him to. You leave him alone, you hear me? You leave both of us alone."

"Gladly. All you have to do is tell me the truth. Did you see Harmon Crane during the two months prior to his death?"

"All *right,* yes, I saw him."

"Where?"

"In San Francisco, at a tavern we frequented while we were married—a former speakeasy on the Embarcadero. I . . . well, we bumped into each other there one afternoon." That last sentence was a lie: she didn't look at me as she said it.

"Where else did you see him? At Tomales Bay?"

". . . Yes, once."

"Did he invite you up there?"

"No. I . . . knew he'd be there and I decided to drive up."

"For what reason?"

No response.

Money, I thought. And she just wasn't going to talk about money. I asked her, "Did anything happen on that visit? Anything unusual?"

"Unusual," she said, and her mouth quirked into an unpleasant little sneer. "He had a woman with him."

"His wife, you mean? Amanda?"

"Hardly. *Another* woman."

127

"Do you know who she was?"

"No." The sneer again. "He didn't introduce us."

"Maybe she was just a casual visitor. . . ."

"They were in bed together when I arrived," Mrs. Brown said. "I wouldn't call that casual, would you?"

"No," I said, "I wouldn't."

"My Lord, the look on Mr. Crane's face when I walked in!" There was a malicious glint in her eyes now; you could tell she was relishing the memory. "I'll never forget it. It was priceless."

"What happened after that?"

"Nothing happened. Mr. Crane took me aside and begged me not to tell anyone about his sordid little affair."

"Is that the word he used, 'affair'?"

"I don't remember what he called it. That was what it *was*."

"Did he offer any explanation?"

"No. The explanation is obvious, isn't it?"

"Maybe. Did you agree not to tell anyone?"

"Reluctantly."

"Did you keep your promise?"

"Of course I kept it."

"Do you remember what day this happened? The date?"

"No, not exactly."

"The month?"

"October, I think. Several weeks before his suicide."

"Before or after the big earthquake?"

". . . Before. A day or two before."

"Did you see or talk to Crane again after that day?"

Hesitation. "I don't remember," she said.

The money again, I thought. "What about the woman? Did you see or talk to *her* again?"

"I *never* spoke to her, not a word. Or saw her again."

"Can you recall what she looked like? I assume you saw her up close that day."

"I saw *all* of her up close, the little tart," Mrs. Brown said. She laughed with malicious humor. "Red hair, white

128

skin with freckles all over . . . hardly any bosom. I can't imagine what Mr. Crane saw in her."

I could say the same about you, lady, I thought. "How old was she, would you say?"

"Under forty."

"Had you ever seen her before that day?"

"No."

"So you don't know where she lived."

"I have no idea. Nor do I care." She glanced at a map-faced clock on the mantel above the fireplace and then gave the globe another aggravated spin. "I've said enough, I'm not going to answer any more of your questions. Please go away."

Her jaw had a stubborn set now; I wasn't going to get anything else out of her. I said, "All right, I won't bother you any longer," and got up and went into the entrance hall. She followed me to the door, stood holding it as I stepped out onto the porch.

Turning, I said, "Thanks for your time, Mrs. Br—"

"Go to hell," she said and slammed the door in my face.

On my way back to the city I put together what I had so far. It wasn't much, really, and what there was of it was open to more than one interpretation. But plenty of solid inferences could be drawn from it just the same.

Harmon Crane was married to a frigid woman. He met the redhead somewhere, San Francisco, Tomales Bay, wherever, and they became lovers. Dancer had told me he didn't think Crane was seeing another woman, but Dancer was a drunk and you can't always trust a drunk's memory or perceptions. I was inclined to believe Mrs. Brown's story of walking in on her ex-husband and the redhead; there had been too much nasty pleasure in her voice for it to have been a fabrication.

All right. Mrs. Brown had been pestering Crane for money, a loan for some purpose or other; Crane kept refusing her. On that score I believed Dancer. But then Ellen Corneal had walked in on Crane and the redhead, and all of a sudden

she had something on him, a little leverage to pry loose that "loan" she'd been after—the $2,000 he'd withdrawn from his savings account on November 6, 1949, some ten days after his return from Tomales Bay. No wonder Mrs. Brown hadn't wanted to talk about the money angle. Technically she was guilty of blackmail and she knew it.

So far, so good. But now there were gaps, missing facts, that still had to be filled in. Assuming it was the red-haired woman's bones Emil Corda and I had found yesterday—and that wasn't a safe assumption yet—what had happened at the cabin the day of, or the day after, the earthquake? A fight of some kind between Crane and the redhead? An accidental death? A premeditated murder? And who was she in the first place? And why had Crane apparently covered up her death by burying her body in the fissure?

If you accepted Crane's culpability, the rest of it seemed cut and dried. He came back from Tomales, he began brooding and drinking heavily—a natural enough reaction, considering he was a sensitive and basically decent man. Then Ellen Corneal blackmailed him for the $2,000: more fuel for his depression and guilt. He finally reached a point on December 10 where it all became intolerable, and he put that .22 of his to his temple and blew himself away.

Simple. The suicide motive explained at last.

Then why didn't I believe it?

Damn it, why did it seem *wrong* somehow?

FIFTEEN

When I got back to the office Eberhardt was gone again and there was another typed note on my desk. This one read:

I talked to DeKalb. Looks like those bones you found are a woman's. Lab found woman's wedding ring, one-carat diamond in gold setting, on a finger bone. Victim was a small adult, probably between 25 and 50, but that's all they can determine so far. Skull may have been crushed prior to burial of body but they're not sure enough to make it official. Unofficially DeKalb thinks it might be homicide connected to your case. He expects to be in touch.

Items buried with bones as follows: four keys on metal ring, cigarette case (no monogram), woman's compact, gold brooch with two small safires (sp?), remains of metal rattail comb, remains of fountain pen, two metal buckles. DeKalb figures all this stuff contents of victim's purse.

You had one call, same pesty woman who called before. Said you'd know who she was and she'd call again. Women.

I sat down and looked out the window at the eddies of fog that obscured the city. Yeah, I thought, women. I didn't want to talk to Mrs. Kiskadon again and I hoped she wouldn't call back while I was here; it would only be more of the same I'd gotten from her up in the park.

I quit thinking about her and thought instead about the woman's wedding ring, one-carat diamond in a gold setting. Harmon Crane's red-haired lover had been married, it seemed. To someone he knew? To a stranger? No way of telling yet. And either way, that kind of affair happens all too often; it didn't have to mean anything significant, to have a direct bearing on the woman's death.

I pulled the phone over and dialed Stephen Porter's number. But it was late afternoon and he just didn't seem to be available at this time of day: no answer. On impulse I looked up Yank-'Em-Out Yankowski's home number and called that. The housekeeper answered. I identified myself,

she said just a minute and went away; when she came back, after a good *three* minutes, she said Mr. Yankowski wasn't home and hung up on me. Uh-huh, I thought. I had figured the old son of a bitch for a grudge-holder and that was what he was.

The phone and I stared at each other for a time. I was debating whether or not I ought to call DeKalb and tell him about the red-haired woman. But there didn't seem to be much point in it just yet. I still had no idea who the woman might have been; for that matter I couldn't even be certain that it was the redhead's bones we'd found yesterday. Some *other* woman's, maybe. Hell, Crane might have had a steady stream of women up there at Tomales Bay, Dancer's opinion notwithstanding. Better to keep on digging on my own. I had more incentive than DeKalb did anyway: I was getting paid for this specific job, and I was a lot more interested in what had happened in late October of 1949 than he was.

I stared out the window some more. Would Amanda Crane have any idea who the red-haired woman had been? Not likely. From all indications she had worshipped her husband; if she'd had any inkling that he was having an affair or affairs, particularly in view of the fact that her frigidity was the probable cause, she was the type of woman who would have put on blinders and refused to admit the truth even to herself. And her mental state being what it was now, it would be cruel to subject her to that kind of questioning. Not that I could even get to see her again, what with that niece of hers on guard. . . .

The niece, I thought. Would *she* know anything about Harmon Crane's extracurricular activities? She couldn't be more than fifty, which made her a teenager when Crane had died; but teenagers are just as perceptive as adults sometimes—and sometimes even nosier—and there was also the possibility that she had picked up knowledge later on, from Mrs. Crane or from someone else.

What was the niece's name again? It took me a few seconds to remember that it was Dubek, Marilyn Dubek. Short-term memory loss—another indicator of creeping old age. I

got the number from Information and dialed it, the idea being to determine whether or not she was home yet. If she'd answered I would have said, "Sorry, wrong number," and hung up and then driven over to Berkeley for the third time in two days. But she didn't answer. Nobody answered.

Temporary impasse.

I decided it was just as well. After four now—almost quitting time. And rush-hour traffic would be turning the bridge approaches into parking lots at this very minute. Who needed to breathe exhaust fumes for an hour or more? Who needed to put up with idiot drivers? Who needed to go to Berkeley to talk about a dead redhead when a live redhead would soon be available in Diamond Heights? Who needed the company of Petunia Pig when the company of Kerry Wade could be had instead?

I closed up half an hour early and hied myself straight to Diamond Heights.

Kerry and I went to a movie down at Ghirardelli Square. It was a mystery movie—"a nightmarish thriller in the grand tradition of Alfred Hitchcock," according to the ads. It was a film to give you nightmares, all right. And both it and its damned ads were a lie.

Filmmakers these days seem to equate suspense with gore: you're supposed to sit there damp-palmed and full of anticipation for the next gusher of blood, the next beheading, the next Technicolor disembowelment. Hitchcock knew different; every *film noir* director in the forties and fifties knew different. Character and atmosphere and mood are the true elements of suspense, cinematic or literary; it's what you *don't* see, what you're forced to imagine, that keeps you poised on the edge of your seat. Not blood, for Christ's sake. Not exposed entrails and rolling heads. Not human depravity of the worst sort.

Seven minutes into this piece of crap, the first bloody slashing took place. One minute later, while it was still going on, we got up and walked out. I've seen too much blood and

133

carnage in my life as it is—*real* blood, *real* carnage. I don't need to be reminded of all the torn flesh, all the violated humanity, all the shattered hopes and futile dreams, all the goddamn waste. And I don't need my guts tied into knots by phony bullshit special effects that make a mockery of violent death and a mockery of its victims.

I said all of this to Kerry after we were outside the theater. I was pretty steamed up and when I get angry I tend to rant a little. Usually she just lets me rant without saying much, Kerry being of the opinion that if somebody is going to throw a tantrum, he ought to do it and be done with it. Very rational, my lady, which can be annoying as hell sometimes. This time, however, she did some ranting of her own; she doesn't like splatter movies any more than I do, especially the ones that employ name actors and hide behind the guise of "thrillers in the grand tradition of Alfred Hitchcock."

We went over to my place, ranting all the way, and had a couple of drinks to get rid of the bad taste, and then ate leftover roast and watched *I Wake Up Screaming* on the tube. *That*, by God, was a suspenseful film. Even Victor Mature had turned in a halfway decent performance for a change.

I asked Kerry to stay the night again—we wouldn't be seeing each other tomorrow night because she'd made other plans—but she declined. She had to be up and at the office early in the morning, she said. Besides, she said, we had been making love altogether too often lately. All that exertion was bad for my heart, she said, an old fellow like me.

Her cockeyed humor again. But I was not amused.

After she left, the old fellow doddered off to bed and reread the first three chapters of *Axe of Mercy*. It had been written during World War II, and it was all about fifth columnists, the black market in rubber goods and gas-rationing coupons, a fat farm called the Spread Shed, and the "Mercy Fund for War Widows" that was anything but. Most of the characters were zany, including the fifth columnists and black-marketeers, and there were all sorts of humorous scenes, descriptions, and dialogue. The last time I'd read it, a few

years back, it had struck me as hilarious farce. This time I was no more amused than I had been at the splatter movie or at Kerry's levity.

Somehow Harmon Crane just wasn't funny anymore.

Five minutes after I arrived at the office on Friday morning, an attorney I knew named Dick Marsten rang up with a job offer: a female witness in a criminal case of his had disappeared and he wanted me to track her down. I would have liked to lay it off on Eberhardt, but he wasn't in yet—as usual—and Marsten had to be in court at eleven. So I said all right, I'd come to his office right away and pick up the details. Never turn down a paying job, especially not when the only other one you've got is as iffy as the Harmon Crane investigation.

I spent forty-five minutes with Marsten. Then I returned to the office and made some calls to start the skip-trace working. Eberhardt still hadn't come in; he'd either gone directly out on the job—he had a skip-trace of his own that he'd been gnawing at since last week—or he'd taken another day off to further mollify the Footwear Queen. If it was the latter we were going to have a talk, Eb and I. Whether he got offended again or not.

By the time I called Stephen Porter, it was almost noon. He was in and as willing to help as ever; the only thing was, he didn't have anything to tell me. He couldn't remember any redheaded woman with milk-white skin and freckles who had been acquainted with the Cranes; in fact he seemed surprised and a little shocked that Crane had been having an affair with anyone. As far as he'd been aware, Crane had been devoted to Amanda. I didn't say anything to him about her frigidity; it wasn't the kind of knowledge that ought to be casually repeated.

I walked over to a chain restaurant on Van Ness, ate a soggy tuna-salad sandwich and drank some iced tea that tasted as if it had been made with dishwater, and walked back again. Still no Eberhardt. I called Marilyn Dubek's number.

No answer. I debated calling Yankowski's home again and decided it would be a waste of time. I looked up the numbers of the novelist and the former confession writer who had known Crane, and called them, and that *was* a waste of time; neither man remembered a freckled redhead in connection with Harmon Crane.

If I had a number for Russ Dancer, I thought, I'd try picking his brain again. But I didn't have a number for him. Or did I? I dialed San Mateo County Information and asked for the number of Mama Luz's Pink Flamingo Tavern. Dancer was there, all right; but a fat lot of good that did me. He was already "about half shit-faced," as he put it, and if he'd ever met the mysterious redhead he couldn't dredge up the memory from the alcoholic bog it was mired in.

I tried Marilyn Dubek again. Busy signal this time; I took that as an encouraging sign, puttered around for ten minutes setting up a file for the Marsten skip-trace, and then redialed her number. Four rings and La Dubek's voice said, "Hello? Marie, is that you?" I said, "Wrong number," and hung up and went to get my hat and coat. Petunia Peg was somebody I would have to talk to in person if I was going to get anything from her other than short shrift.

The sun was shining in Berkeley this afternoon, which was more than you could say for San Francisco. Not that it was any warmer over there; a strong cold wind was blowing. The wind had tugged leaves and twigs off the trees lining Linden Street and carpeted the pavement with them; more leaves covered the Dubek lawn, littered the porch stairs. As soon as the wind stopped blowing, I thought, she would be out here with a broom—or maybe her vacuum cleaner—to tidy up. She was just that type.

She answered promptly when I leaned on the doorbell. Her dyed black hair was up in curlers, her fat lips looked as if they had been stained with blueberry juice, and she was wearing a housedress that was as colorful and puckish as a page from the Sunday funnies. In one hand she carried a saucepan

full of stringbeans, holding it tight-fisted like a weapon. She was quite a sight. If there had ever been a Porky in her life he had probably run off screaming years ago, in self-defense.

She glared at me, said, "Oh, it's you again," and got ready to shut the door in my face. "You can't see my aunt. She's not seeing anybody—"

"I didn't come to see Mrs. Crane," I said quickly, "I came to see you."

"Me? What for?"

"To ask you some questions."

"About Harmon Crane, I suppose. Well, I'm not answering any questions about him, not for you or any other fan."

"I'm not a fan."

"Writer, then."

"I'm not a writer."

"Well? Then what are you?"

"A private detective."

If that surprised her she didn't show it. Suspicion made her little pig eyes glitter. "Prove it," she said.

I proved it with the photostat of my license. "Now can we talk, Miss Dubek?"

"It's Mrs. Dubek, if you don't mind. Talk about what?"

"About Harmon Crane."

"Listen," she said, "what is this? Who hired you to come around here bothering us?"

"Michael Kiskadon."

"Oh, so that's it. Claiming to be Harmon's son. I don't believe it for a minute. Not a minute, you hear me?"

"I hear you, Miss Dubek."

"It's *Missus* Dubek."

I said, "Do you have any idea why Harmon Crane shot himself?"

"What?" she said. Then she said, "I'm not going to answer that. I don't have to answer your questions, why should I?" And she started to close the door again.

"If you don't answer my questions," I said, "you might have to answer the same ones from the police."

"What?"

"The police, Miss Dubek."

"Missus, missus, how many times do I have to— Police? Why should the police want to ask me questions?"

"You and Mrs. Crane both."

"That's ridiculous, I never heard of such a thing. Why, for heaven's sake?"

"Because of some bones that were found the other day at Tomales Bay. Human bones, buried at the site of the cabin Harmon Crane rented up there. A woman's bones."

She gawped at me slack-jawed. Behind her, somewhere in the house, Amanda Crane's voice called, "Marilyn? Do we have company, dear?" The Dubek blinked, glanced over her shoulder, said in a tolerable bellow, "No, Auntie, it's all right, you go back and rest," and glared at me again. "Now see what you've done," she said, using a snarl this time, and then crowded past me onto the porch and shut the door behind her.

"I'm sorry, Miss Dubek, but I—"

She made an exasperated sound through her teeth. "You're doing that on purpose," she said, "calling me *Miss* Dubek like that, trying to get me all flustered. But it won't work, you hear me? It won't work!"

"Yes, ma'am."

"Now what's this about bones? A woman's bones, you said?"

"That's right. Buried in an old earthquake fissure at Tomales Bay. Probably right after one of the bigger quakes— the one in 1949, for instance."

"You don't think *Harmon* buried those bones? My God!"

"It wasn't bones that were buried. It was the body of a woman."

"That's crazy. Harmon? Harmon and some woman?"

"You don't believe that's possible?"

"Of course not. Harmon wasn't a philanderer like that lowlife *I* married; he and Auntie were devoted to each

138

other." She scowled and waggled the saucepan at me. "What woman are you talking about? Whose bones?"

"The police aren't sure yet. But she was probably a redhead, the kind with milk-white skin and freckles. Would you know if the Cranes knew anyone who fits that description?"

"Redhead, you say? Milk-white skin?"

"And freckles. Lots of freckles."

"How do you know all of that, anyway? What she looked like? If it was just bones that were found—"

"The police have ways," I said cryptically. "About that redhead, Miss Dubek . . ."

"You stop that now. I won't tell you again, it's missus—missus, missus, missus!"

"About that redhead, Mrs. Dubek."

Another scowl, but it was in concentration this time. Pretty soon she said, "I remember I went up to Tomales Bay with Auntie one summer to see Harmon, 1948 or 1949, I was just a girl at the time. We had lunch with some other people; I think one of the women was a redhead . . . yes, I'm sure she was. Red hair and white skin and freckles."

"Do you remember her name?"

"Some Italian name. Her *last* name, I mean. I thought that was funny because she looked Irish—all that red hair, Irish, not Italian. And her first name was . . . let's see . . . Kate, that's it. Kate."

I said, "The last name wouldn't have been Bertolucci, would it?"

"Well, it might have been," she said. "Bertolucci. Mmm, yes, Kate Bertolucci. Her husband was the man who rented Harmon the cabin."

SIXTEEN

My watch read a quarter of four when I drove away from the Dubek house. I could have let a second talk with Angelo Bertolucci slide until tomorrow, or even until Monday; I could have driven back to San Francisco and relaxed with a cold bottle of Miller Lite in my living room. Instead I turned north on the Eastshore Freeway and headed for the Richmond-San Rafael Bridge, the quickest route from Berkeley to Marin County and eventually to Tomales. Bird dog on the scent.

Traffic wasn't bad until I got onto the bridge. Then it began to snarl and it stayed snarled all the way through San Rafael and halfway to Novato. Rush hour, they called it, which was a laugh—the painful kind, like a fart in church. Nobody was rushing this afternoon; nobody ever rushed on the freeways after four P.M. on Friday, good old TGIF. I quit muttering and cursing after a while and resigned myself to doing what I'd avoided doing last night: smelling exhaust fumes, watching out for idiot drivers, and otherwise dealing with the Great American Traffic Jam.

While I crawled along I brooded about the Bertoluccis, Angelo and Kate. It seemed probable that she was the woman Harmon Crane had been having his affair with, the woman Ellen Corneal had caught him in bed with and used for blackmail leverage; and it also seemed probable that those were her bones we'd found at the old cabin site. But identifying her raised plenty of new questions. Had Bertolucci known about the affair? And if he had, had he done anything about it? How had he reacted to his wife's disappearance? How had he explained it to his friends and neighbors?

Bertolucci had the answers to those questions. And maybe he also had the answers to two others, the two big ones: Why had his wife died? Who was responsible? I kept thinking what a queer old duck he was; and I kept remember-

ing the way he'd looked the other day, standing out there in his vegetable patch with his shotgun in one hand and the dead and bloody crow in the other. . . .

At Hamilton Field the traffic began to move more or less normally, and once I got past Novato it thinned out enough so that I could maintain a steady sixty. I quit the freeway in Petaluma, picked up and followed the same two-lane county road I'd taken to Tomales on Wednesday. Dusk had settled when I got there; it was a few minutes before six. The fog was in, thick and restless, pressing down close to the ground so that it filled the hollows and dips and obscured the hilltops. Building and street lights shone pale and indistinct, like daubs of yellow in a hologram seen through gray gauze.

The general store was still open; I turned off Shoreline Highway and stopped in front of it. The same dark-haired girl was behind the counter. I waited until she finished waiting on the only customer in the place and then said to her, "Hi. Remember me?"

"Oh sure," she said. "You're the man who was asking about Mr. Bertolucci the other day."

"Right. I wonder if you could answer a few more questions for me."

"Well . . . I guess so, if I can."

"Mr. Bertolucci used to be married, didn't he?"

"A long time ago, I think. Way before I was born."

"Was his wife's name Kate?"

"Kate. I *think* that was it."

"Do you know what happened to her?"

"Gee, no. She ran off with another man or something. My mother could tell you. Do you want to talk to her?"

"Where would I find her?"

"She's here, back in the storeroom. I'll get her for you."

She left the counter and disappeared into the rear of the store. Trusting people up here in the country; I could have made off with the entire cash register, not to mention its contents. Too long in the city, that was my trouble. Too many

141

dealings with criminal types. If I lived in a place like Tomales, such thoughts would probably never even enter my head.

The girl came back with an older, graying version of herself, dressed in a leather apron over a man's shirt and a pair of Levi's. The older woman said her name was Martha Kramer and I gave her my name but not the fact that I was a detective; I told her I was a genealogical researcher trying to track down information on Angelo Bertolucci's wife, Kate, for a client in San Francisco.

"Oh, I see," she said, and nodded.

"I went to see Mr. Bertolucci on Wednesday afternoon, after I spoke to your daughter. He wasn't very cooperative, I'm afraid. He seemed . . . well, kind of odd."

"Odd is the word for it," Mrs. Kramer agreed.

"Just as I was leaving he went out into his yard and shot a crow. With a twelve-gauge shotgun."

A faint wry smile. "He does that sometimes. It used to frighten his neighbors but no one pays much attention anymore."

"He must have lived alone for a long time," I said.

"Ever since Mrs. Bertolucci left him. That must have been . . . oh, more than thirty years ago."

"October 1949? That's as far as I've been able to trace her."

"I believe it was 1949, yes."

"You say she left him. Divorced him, you mean?"

"No. Ran off."

"With another man?"

"Evidently."

"She and Mr. Bertolucci didn't get along, then."

"Not very well. Fought all the time."

"Over anything in particular?"

"His general cussedness, my mother used to say."

"Did the fights ever become physical?"

"A time or two. He was free with his fists."

"A violent man?"

"Well, you saw what he does to crows."

142

"Would you have any idea who Mrs. Bertolucci ran off with?"

"Lord, no. I was only a child then."

"So her affair wasn't common knowledge."

"No. But people weren't surprised, the way he treated her."

"It *was* common knowledge, though, that she'd run off?"

"He admitted it himself, more than once."

"Did he seem upset by the fact?"

"I suppose he was. Who wouldn't be?"

"And he never remarried?"

"No. Never set foot out of Tomales since, that I know of."

I took out my notebook and made some squiggles in it, mostly for show. "What can you tell me about Mrs. Bertolucci?"

"Well, let's see," Mrs. Kramer said. "Her maiden name was Dunlap; she was Irish . . . but you must already know that."

"Mmm."

"I think Mr. Bertolucci met her through her father. He ran a plumbing supply company in Santa Rosa . . . no, he was a plumbing contractor, that's right. Used to hunt out here before all the land was posted, and Mr. Bertolucci made some of his trophies. He died a year or so before Mrs. Bertolucci disappeared."

"Did she have other relatives in Santa Rosa?"

"Not that I know of. You haven't been able to find any?"

"Not so far. Did she have any close friends here in Tomales, someone I might talk to?"

"Well . . . her best friend was Bernice Toland, but Bernice died several years back. Kate wrote her a note before she left town, said she was going away with a man; that was the first Bernice knew about it, apparently."

"Bernice never heard from her again?"

"No, never."

"Is there anybody else I might see?"

"A couple of others, I suppose, but I don't think they can tell you much more than I have."

I took their names and addresses, thanked Mrs. Kramer and her daughter, and went out to my car. For a time I sat there watching the fog swirl across the deserted highway, mulling over what I had just learned. It all seemed to fit. And what seemed to fit, too, was the way Angelo Bertolucci had dealt with his wife's disappearance—the way a man would if he had something to hide, if he'd had something to do with the disappearing.

Bertolucci was the one I wanted to talk to now; the two casual acquaintances of his wife's could wait. I started the car and swung out onto Dillon Beach Road and drove up toward Hill Street. The fog was so thick my headlight beams seemed to break off against the wall of it, smearing yellow across the gray but not penetrating it. I had to drive at a virtual crawl; I couldn't see more than twenty yards ahead.

The street sign came up out of the mist—Hill Street— and then the joining of its unpaved surface with the road I was on. Out of habit I put on the turn signal just before I started the right-hand swing.

There was a rush of thrumming sound in the fog ahead, and all at once a car came hurtling out of Hill Street, just a dark shape, no lights, like some sort of phantom materializing. I let out a yell, jerked the wheel hard right, came down on the brake pedal; the rear end broke loose and for a second or two I lost control, skidding on the rutted gravelly surface. The other driver had swerved too, which prevented a head-on collision, but as it was his car scraped along my left rear fender and booted my clunker around until it was slanted sideways across the road. The bump put an end to the skid, at least, and let me get the thing stopped. Meanwhile the other car bounced off, careened out onto Dillon Beach Road, and was almost immediately swallowed up by the gray mist. It had all happened so fast that I couldn't identify the make or model or even its color.

I shouted, "You stupid goddamn son of a bitch *bastard!*"

144

at the top of my lungs, which wasn't very smart: coming on top of my fright, it might have given me a coronary. As it was, all I got was a raw throat and no satisfaction. I sat there for a minute or so, until I calmed down. Sat in silence, with nothing moving around me except the fog. The nearest house, the one with the Confederate flag for a window curtain, showed no light; the driver of the other car, drunk or sober, crazy or just plain witless, probably lived there. Christ!

The engine had stalled; I started it again and got the car straightened out and drove it up to Bertolucci's front gate. The palms of my hands and my armpits were damp, and when I got out the fog turned the dampness clammy and cold. Shivering, I went to the rear fender and shined my flashlight on it to check the damage. Foot-long scrape and a dent the size of my fist; the paint along the scrape was black.

I tossed the flashlight onto the front seat, muttering to myself, and then gave my attention to Bertolucci's house. Dim light illuminated its front and side windows, blurred by the fog. If he'd heard the collision he hadn't been curious enough to come out to investigate. I pushed through the gate and made my way through the tangle of weeds and mist-damp lilac bushes to the porch. The same sign still hung from the door: *Ring Bell and Come In.* I followed instructions, just as I had on Wednesday.

Bertolucci's display room was empty except for the poised animals and birds staring blankly with their glass eyes. The musty, gamy smell seemed even stronger tonight, overlain with the moist brackish odor of the fog. It was cold in there too; the old wood-stove in one corner was unlit and there weren't any furnace vents or registers that I could see.

"Mr. Bertolucci?"

One of the old house's joints creaked. Or maybe it was a mouse or something larger scurrying around inside the walls. Otherwise, silence.

I walked past the stuffed raccoon sitting up on its hind paws, the owl about to take flight with its rabbit dinner, the two chicken hawks mounted combatively on pedestals. The

sound in the wall came again; the stillness that followed it had an empty quality, the kind you feel in abandoned buildings.

"Mr. Bertolucci?"

The faint echo of my voice, nothing else.

The door at the rear, behind the rodents on display in the glass cases, stood partially ajar; more pale lamplight came from the other side. I moved through an opening between the cases and shoved the door all the way open.

Bertolucci's workroom. An organized clutter: big work-table in the middle, labeled containers on a shelf underneath that held clay, plaster of paris, varnish, something called tow; tools hanging from wall racks; battered chest of drawers with each drawer labeled in a spidery hand, one of them with the word *Eyes;* a chopping block, a carborundum wheel, an electric saw, a box overflowing with cotton batting, spools of thread and twine; tins of wax, paint, gasoline, formaldehyde, and wood alcohol; a tub of what looked to be corn meal. Dusty stacks of wooden shields and panels and mounts of various sizes, teetering in one corner; a jumble of old pieces of wire strewn in another. All this and more, shadowed and fusty in the pale light from a ceiling globe.

But no Bertolucci.

I called his name again, got the same faint echo and the same silence, and went at an angle to another door on my right. This one gave onto the kitchen, sink piled high with crusty dishes, ants crawling in a trail of spilled sugar on the floor. No Bertolucci here either. Two more doors opened off the kitchen, one to the rear of the house and one toward the front. I decided to try the rear one first, and started toward it, and that was when I first smelled the faint lingering stench of spent gunpowder.

The muscles across my shoulders bunched up; my stomach jumped, knotted, brought up the taste of bile. No, I thought, ah Christ, not again, not another one. But I went ahead anyway, pushed open the door and eased through it.

Narrow areaway, opening onto a laundry porch. And Bertolucci lying back there, blood all over him, blood on the

146

floor and splashed on one wall—real blood, not the fake stuff they use in those damned death-mocking splatter movies. Torn and blackened and gaping hole where his chest had once been, and that was real too, and so was his twelve-guage shotgun on the floor to one side. Point blank range: the powder blackening said that. And buckshot, not birdshot.

The back door was wide open; fog reached in like searching fingers, skeletal and gray and grave-cold. That was why I hadn't been able to smell the burnt gunpowder until I got to the kitchen: the wind had blown most of the odor away, even though the weapon couldn't have been fired more than a few minutes ago. The blood was still fresh, glistening wet red in the spill of light from the kitchen.

Driver of that black car, I thought. Has to be. Not a crazy kid, not a Friday night drunk—a murderer fleeing the scene of a just-committed homicide. And if I'd come straight here instead of stopping at the general store, maybe it wouldn't have been committed at all. . . .

That's crap, I thought, you know better than that. Then I thought: If I stand here any longer I'll puke. I backed up and let the door wobble shut, blocking out the carnage in the areaway. But it was still there behind my eyes, all that blood, all that ruined flesh, as I stumbled back through the house to find a phone and call the sheriff's department.

SEVENTEEN

It was after nine before the authorities, in the person of Sergeant Chet DeKalb, allowed me to leave Tomales. De-Kalb had come out even though he was off duty, because I had asked for him specifically. He wasn't pleased at having been yanked away from dinner with his family—he lived in

Terra Linda and it was a long drive from there to Tomales—but he didn't take it out on me. He was polite; and when he saw the way Bertolucci's murder shaped up he even permitted a spark of interest to show through his stoicism.

We did our talking in the display room, with those stuffed things looking on. Lab men, photographers, uniformed deputies, the county coroner paraded in and out, performing the grim aftermath ritual of violent death. Outside, knots of local residents shivered in the fog, as indistinct when you had glimpses of them as half-formed wraiths. The revolving red light on the county ambulance made one of the windows alternately light up with a crimson glow and then go dark, like the winking of a bloody eye.

I told DeKalb everything I knew about Bertolucci, everything I had suspected about him and his connection with those bones. "But now I don't know," I said. "What happened here tonight . . . it confuses the hell out of things."

"Not necessarily," DeKalb said. "There doesn't have to be a correlation between your investigation and Bertolucci's death."

"Doesn't have to be, no."

"But you think there is."

"I don't know what to think right now."

"Could have been a prowler," DeKalb said. "Bertolucci caught him, tried to scare him off with the shotgun; they struggled, the gun went off, bang the old man's dead."

"Yeah," I said.

"Or somebody local had a grudge against him. You said nobody seemed to like him much."

"Why *now*, though? The same week a thirty-five-year-old can of worms opened up."

"Coincidences happen."

"Sure. I've had a few happen to me over the years. But this time . . . I don't know, it doesn't feel right that way."

"Hunches," DeKalb said. "You can't always trust 'em."

"Granted. Hell, I don't see how the murder can be tied up with Harmon Crane and the missing wife, either."

148

"Anybody you can think of who might have had a motive?"

"That's just it, I can't think of a single person or a single motive—not after all these years."

"You tell anybody your suspicions about Bertolucci and his wife?"

"No. I only found out about her this afternoon, and I came straight here afterward."

"Who told you about the wife?"

"Woman in Berkeley—Marilyn Dubek, the niece of Crane's widow. But she's fat, fifty, and a housefrau; the idea of her following me here and blowing Bertolucci away is ridiculous."

"What about the widow?"

"No way. Late sixties and mentally incompetent ever since her husband's suicide."

"Well, maybe the Dubek woman told somebody else what she told you after you left."

"Maybe. But I got here as fast as anybody could in rush-hour traffic, and I was in the general store no more than fifteen minutes. Whoever killed Bertolucci pretty much had to have arrived at the same time I did and probably a while earlier. Don't you think?"

"Seems that way," he agreed.

"I don't suppose any of the neighbors saw the car?"

DeKalb shook his head. "Nobody home at two of the houses. Old woman who lives in the other place up the way was cooking her supper; besides that, she's half-blind."

I said, "You know, if this was the perpetrator's first visit here, he might have had to stop over in the business section to ask directions."

"Already thought of that. Officers are checking it now. Let's get back to your investigation. Did you tell anybody about your first meeting with Bertolucci?"

"Just my client."

"Michael Kiskadon," DeKalb said, nodding. "I don't suppose you'd consider *him* a candidate?"

I hesitated, remembering what I'd thought yesterday morning after talking to Kiskadon on the phone—that if his wife didn't get him some psychiatric help pretty soon, he was liable to come unwrapped. And then what? I'd wondered. What happens to a guy like Kiskadon when he starts to unravel? Well, murder was one thing that happens to head cases; the sheer terrifying number of lunatics running around committing atrocities these days was proof of that. But something had to trigger a homicidal act, and I had told Kiskadon nothing about Angelo Bertolucci that could have induced a murderous rage. Besides, there was Kiskadon's physical condition: he was weak, he could barely get around unaided, he seldom left the house even for short periods. I could no more envision him driving all the way up to Tomales to confront Bertolucci than I could Marilyn Dubek.

I said these things to DeKalb and he concurred. But he felt that a talk with Kiskadon was indicated just the same. So did I, even though I did not relish the prospect; and I thought that for Kiskadon's sake, it would be better if I got to him first.

Before DeKalb let me leave, he took down the names and addresses of all the other people I had interviewed this past week, including Russ Dancer. Methodical and thorough, that was Chet DeKalb—qualities possessed by all good cops, public and private. He also sent one of the lab men out to take scrapings of the black paint from the banged-up fender of my car. And when I drove away a few minutes later, past the morbid wraiths huddled together in the mist, the lab guy and one of the deputies were using portable crime-scene floodlights to comb the area near the Dillon Beach Road intersection, looking for anything that might have come off the black car during the collision.

The fog stayed thick and roiling, retarding my speed, until I neared Petaluma; then it lifted into a high overcast and I was able to make better time. It was twenty of eleven when I came across the Golden Gate Bridge, and eleven on the nose when I walked into my flat. I was tired and I felt crawly and I

wanted a shower and some sleep. My stomach was giving me hell too; so even though I had no appetite, and before I did anything else, I ate some mortadella and a wedge of gorgonzola and a carton of pineapple cottage cheese. Which was a bad idea, as it turned out. The stuff congealed in my stomach for some reason and gave me the twin devilments of heartburn and gas.

I lay in bed belching and farting and trying to sleep. But I couldn't get rid of the persistent image of Bertolucci's buckshot-savaged corpse, of all that glistening blood. And I couldn't stop thinking about the *why* of his death, either. If it was connected with what happened in 1949, and my gut instincts still said that it was, the reason for the killing escaped me completely.

Motive, motive, what was the damned motive?

I was up at seven-ten in the morning, gritty-eyed and headachy and depressed. It took a long shower, followed by three cups of strong coffee, to clear away the remnants of the nightmares that had plagued my sleep. It was always that way after I stumbled on violent death: the bad dreams, the day-after depression. Some cops had become inured to the residue of violence; I never had, which was one of the reasons I had quit the force twenty-five years ago to open my own agency. No corpses to deal with then, I'd thought; just the pain and tears of the living. Well, I'd been wrong—Christ, how wrong I'd been. I had seen more death these past twenty-five years than I ever would have if I had stayed on the cops.

I called Kerry's number at eight-thirty. No answer. That stirred me up a little, until I remembered that it was Saturday: she went jogging on Saturday mornings, sometimes in Golden Gate Park, sometimes around Lake Merced, sometimes down on the Marina Green. She wasn't one of those jogging fanatics; she didn't run every day, she didn't run fifty miles a week, she just ran on Saturdays for exercise. I forgave her for it, now that she had quit trying to coerce *me* into running with her. Everybody is entitled to one small lunacy.

151

So I called Eberhardt's house, and he was't home either. *That* nettled me. Over at Wanda's again, probably; spending too damn much time with her since the Il Roccaforte fiasco, soothing her ruffled feathers. Or more likely stroking her unfeathered chest. Neglecting his work, mooning around like a lovesick jerk—he was beginning to annoy the hell out of me, and the next time I saw him I was going to tell him so. I considered calling him at Wanda's and decided I didn't want to talk to her. Nor him very badly, for that matter. Let him read about Bertolucci's death in the papers.

As early as it was, I went ahead and dialed Kiskadon's number. I figured he would probably be up by now, and I wanted to reach him before DeKalb did. He was up, all right—he answered right away—and he sounded neither happy nor unhappy to hear from me. But he didn't know about Bertolucci yet or he would have said something when I asked him if I could stop by. He wanted to know if I had news; I said yes but it would be better if we discussed it in person; he told me to come over any time. There was a bitter, hopeless note in his voice that I didn't like.

It was foggy on Golden Gate Heights; you could barely see the tops of the trees over in the park. Nobody was out and around. The whole area had a gray, abandoned look, like a neighborhood in a plague city. Some mood I was in when that sort of thought crossed my mind.

Lynn Kiskadon answered the door. Pale-featured except for dark circles under her eyes, and bulgy again in another pair of too-tight Calvin Klein jeans. Before I could say anything, she stepped out on the porch, pulled the door against its latch, and held it there with one hand.

She said, "He's waiting in his den. He thinks you've got bad news—I can tell by the way he looks."

"I'm afraid I have."

"Oh God, I knew it," she said, "I knew it." The words were like a lament, soft and moaning and edged with self-pity. "What have you found out?"

"I'd rather say it just once, Mrs. Kiskadon."

"He won't want me in the room with the two of you."

"Why not?"

"We had another fight. Wednesday night, after you and I talked in the park. He hasn't said five words to me since."

I didn't say anything.

"I tried to call you on Thursday and again yesterday. I thought . . . I don't know what I thought. I don't know who else to turn to."

"What was the fight about?"

"He won't see a psychiatrist, he won't even talk to his own doctor. He just won't face the truth about himself."

"He sounded depressed on the phone," I said.

"Worse than I've ever seen him. He just sits in his den reading his father's books and stories. Won't eat, won't talk, just sits there until all hours. Do you *have* to tell him this news of yours?"

"I don't have a choice."

"It's really so bad?"

"Not to you or me. But it will be to him."

"Then don't tell him! God knows what he might do."

"Mrs. Kiskadon, if you're afraid of that gun of his, why don't you get it out of his desk and hide it somewhere?"

"It's in a locked drawer and he has the only key. And he's in the den all the time."

"I've still got to tell him," I said. "If I don't, the Marin County Sheriff's Department will."

"Sheriff's Department? My God, what—"

"We'd better go inside, Mrs. Kiskadon."

She made a little whiny noise, but she let me reach around her and push open the door and prod her gently inside. It was quiet in the house—too quiet to suit me right now. We went through the living room and along the short hall to the door to Kiskadon's den. I knocked and said his name, and from inside he said, "It's open, come ahead," and we went in.

He was sitting in the recliner chair, his cane laid across

his lap, a cold pipe in one corner of his mouth. The table at his elbow was stacked with pulps, issues of *Collier's* and *American Magazine* and *The Saturday Evening Post*, three of the Johnny Axe novels. He didn't look any different than he had the last time I'd been here—except for his eyes. There was no animation in them; they were as dark and lightless as burned-out bulbs. And the whites were flecked and streaked with blood.

He said, "You'll excuse me if I don't get up. My leg's bothering me today."

I moved toward him by a couple of steps, and Lynn Kiskadon shut the door and stood back against it. Kiskadon looked at her, the kind of look that told her silently and bitterly to get out. She said, "I'm staying, Michael. I have a right to hear this too."

He didn't answer her. As far as he was concerned, she *had* gone out. He said to me, with the bitterness in his voice, "Glad tidings, I trust?"

"I'm sorry, no."

"I didn't think so. Well? I'm ready."

I told him. The evident affair between Harmon Crane and Kate Bertolucci, my suspicions, Angelo Bertolucci's murder—not softening any of it but not going into unnecessary detail either. Once, when I first mentioned the murder, Lynn Kiskadon made the little whiny noise again behind me. Otherwise the only sound in the room was my own voice. Kiskadon didn't speak or move or display any reaction to what I said; his face was as blank as his eyes.

When I finished there were maybe ten seconds of silence. Then he said, "So my father was an adulterer and a murderer. Well, well." No bitterness in his tone now. No emotion at all. The flat, genderless voice of a programmed machine.

"We don't know that he killed anyone, Mr. Kiskadon."

"Don't we? It seems plain enough to me."

"Not to me," I said. "Bertolucci could just as easily have been the one responsible for his wife's death. Maybe even somebody else."

"Just the same, my father had to be involved, didn't he? If he wasn't involved, he wouldn't have become begun drinking so heavily afterward, he wouldn't have become so depressed. He wouldn't have shot himself, now would he?"

"We don't have all the facts yet—"

"Enough to suit me."

"There's still the murder last night," I said.

"I don't care about that."

"You'd better care about it, Mr. Kiskadon. I think Bertolucci was killed because of what happened in 1949."

"Does that make my father any less guilty?"

"I don't know. It might."

"Bullshit," he said.

"You don't seem to understand. This isn't an archeological expedition anymore, it isn't a simple search for the motive in your father's suicide. It's a homicide case now."

"I don't give a damn," he said.

"Is that what you're going to say to Sergeant DeKalb when he shows up?"

"To hell with Sergeant DeKalb. If he wants to arrest me for any reason, let him. I don't care. That's what *you* don't seem to understand. I don't care who killed Bertolucci, I don't care who killed his slut of a wife or why, I don't care about any of it anymore."

"Why not? Just because your father wasn't the kind of man you thought he was?"

No answer. Kiskadon wasn't looking at me either, now. He reached for the canister of tobacco on the table and methodically began to load the bowl of his pipe.

I glanced around at Lynn Kiskadon. Her expression was pleading, helpless; her eyes said, *You see? You see?*

I saw, all right. But there wasn't anything I could do about it, not for him and not for her. What could I do? I was no head doctor; I didn't know the first thing about dealing with the kinds of neuroses running around inside Kiskadon's skull. I was fortunate if I could deal with the ones inside my own.

Kiskadon struck a kitchen match and lit his pipe. When he had it drawing he said, still without looking at me, "I appreciate all you've done, but I won't need your services any longer. Send me a bill for the balance of what I owe you. Or I can write you a check right now if you'd prefer it that way."

Nothing to say to that except, "Have it your way, Mr. Kiskadon. I'll send you a bill." Nothing to do then except to turn and walk out of there, avoiding Mrs. Kiskadon's eyes. And nothing to do after that except to feel twice as shitty and twice as frustrated on the drive back home.

EIGHTEEN

Ten minutes after I came into my flat, just as I was about to call Kerry, the telephone rang. I picked up the receiver and said hello, and there was a wheezing intake of breath followed by a series of fitful coughs. So I knew it was Stephen Porter even before he identified himself.

"That box of Harmon Crane's papers I told you about," he said, panting a little. "I finally found it. It was in the basement, just as I thought, but hidden at the bottom of Adam's old steamer trunk."

"Anything among the papers that might help me?"

"Well, I really can't say. Most of them are manuscript carbons. There are some letters written to Harmon, and some by him, but they seem mostly to be business-related. Of course—" He coughed again. "Of course, I haven't read everything. Perhaps you'll be able to find something useful."

"Perhaps. When can I have a look at them?"

"Right away, if you like. I'd drop the box off to you, but I have a student coming at noon. . . ."

"No, no, I'll come by your studio. Half an hour okay?"

"Yes, fine. I'll be"—more coughing—"I'll be here."

I postponed the call to Kerry and started immediately for North Beach. The weather was better over there and the tourists and Saturday slummers were out in full force; there was no way I was going to find legal street parking. And the nearest garage to Porter's place was blocks away. So I parked in a bus zone down the street from his building, the hell with it.

Porter was wearing the same green smock and the same red bow tie, or at least identical twins to the ones he'd had on the last time I was here: both were spotted with dried clay. He had a cigarette burning in one hand and what breath he had left made burbling noises in his nose and throat.

The box was on one of the clay-smeared worktables, cardboard and largish; the papers jammed into it looked to be mostly yellow foolscap. I asked Porter if he wanted me to sort through them here, and he said, "No, you can take the box with you," and then lapsed into a coughing fit so severe it bent him double and turned his face an apoplectic beet red. I wanted to do something for him but there wasn't anything to do. I just stood there, feeling helpless, until he got his breath back.

"One of my bad days," he said. "Damned emphysema."

Damned cigarettes, I thought.

I carried the box to the studio door. Porter went with me, firing up another Camel on the way. Walking dead man, I thought then. And tried not to let him see the pity I felt when I said good-bye.

Manuscript carbons. Handwritten notes. Typed fragments and unfinished stories. Letters from Crane's New York agent and from the editors of various book and magazine publishers. Carbons of letters from Crane to those same individuals. A few personal letters addressed to Crane. Carbons of his responses and some other personal correspondence. Most of his papers, it seemed, from 1942 until the time of his death.

Sitting at the kitchen table, thinking that Harmon Crane had been something of a pack rat, I finished sorting out the

sheets of stationery and yellow foolscap and then began methodically to wade through them. The manuscript carbons
first: two of the Johnny Axe novels, *Axe for Trouble* and
Don't Axe Me; and more than thirty short stories and novel-
ettes, most of them featuring Johnny Axe, all of them marked
SOLD and bearing both a date and the name of either a pulp
or a slick magazine. I riffled through some of the manuscripts
from 1949. Plenty to interest a collector or a scholar; nothing
to interest a detective. I put the carbons back into the box and
gave my attention to the notes and fragments.

Most of the handwritten notes—none of which were
dated—seemed to be ideas for stories: "Carny owner shot,
geek arrested by cops, Axe hired as new geek—funny or too
bizarre?" The typed sheets were nearly all one and two pages
in length: story openings, descriptions of places and people,
clever bits of dialogue, brief plot synopses. There were also
two longer fragments. The first was headed *Kick Axe!*, ran to
fourteen pages, and appeared to be an early draft of the opening chapter of *Axe and Pains*. I read through it, looking for
Bertolucci's name, but it wasn't there.

The other segment bore a pulpish title—"You Can't Run
Away from Death"—and was a little over eight pages long.
Unfinished pulp story, I thought. But it wasn't. Halfway
through the first page I realized it was something much more
than that.

> Numb with shock, Rick Durbin stared at the
> body on the cabin floor. Carla. It was Carla! Some-
> body had come here while he was in the village buy-
> ing groceries. Somebody had beaten her to death
> with a chunk of stovewood.
>
> Borelli, he thought. It had to be her husband,
> Borelli.
>
> Durbin fell to his knees beside her. He wanted
> to cry but he had no tears. He'd loved her. Or had
> he? He didn't know. He didn't know anything right
> now except that she was dead. Murdered. Lying here

so still, blood shining in her red hair, where only an hour ago she had been so warm and vibrant and alive.

What was he going to do?

What Durbin did, on page 2, was to pick up the body, carry it outside and away from the isolated cabin on a body of water called Anchor Bay, and bury it. In an earthquake fissure: there had been a "terrifying" earthquake the day before. He did that instead of notifying the authorities because he was afraid they would suspect him of the crime. He had no proof the husband, Borelli, had murdered Carla. And he was the cabin's tenant; he was staying there alone. And Carla was another man's wife; *his* wife was back home in San Francisco. Even if he could make the sheriff believe his story, there was the scandal to consider: Durbin was a writer, he had a film deal pending in Hollywood for one of his books, the notoriety would ruin his career.

Durbin went back to the cabin and cleaned the bloodstains off the floor. Then he gathered up Carla's purse and other belongings, put them into the fissure with her body, and used dirt and grass and oyster shells to conceal his handiwork. No one would ever know, he thought; no one had suspected his affair with Carla—except Borelli—because they had been very careful to keep it a secret. There was nothing to connect Carla or her disappearance to him. With her buried, he thought, he was completely safe.

When the job was done he packed his own belongings and drove straight home to San Francisco. But he couldn't forget Carla or what he'd done. Her dead face haunted his dreams, saying over and over, "You told me you loved me. How can you do this to someone you loved?" He couldn't sleep, couldn't work. He thought time and again of returning to Anchor Bay, making a clean breast to the authorities, showing them where he had buried her; but he couldn't find the courage—it was too late, they would never believe him now that so much time had elapsed. He began to drink too

much in a futile effort to drown his guilt and to ward off a
growing paranoia.

Every time the telephone or doorbell rang, Durbin was terrified that it would be the police. Or, almost as bad, that it would be Borelli. Borelli was a
violent man, a dangerous man. And he wasn't stupid. He knew something had been done with Carla's
body. He knew who and why. He might not be satisfied to let it go at that. He might decide to eliminate
the one man who knew the truth, who could put him
in the gas chamber for Carla's murder. What if he
comes here? What if he tries to kill me too? What if
he
          What if

That was where it ended. To Stephen Porter, to me before I began to realize what had happened at Tomales Bay in
October of 1949, these pages would seem to be the beginning
of a pulp story, unsalable and abandoned because it was too
emotional and too immoral for its time; but what it really was
was a pathetic attempt by Crane to purge his demons by fic-
tionalizing the truth—a confession that was never intended to
be read, that his pack-rat tendencies had kept him from de-
stroying after he was no longer able to continue it. Positive
proof of why he had taken his own life later on, all the dark,
bleak, ugly motives: guilt, fear, self-loathing, paranoia. And
maybe he *had* loved Kate Bertolucci, at least a little; maybe
that was part of it too. He not only hadn't had the guts to try
to see her murderer punished, he had tucked her away in the
ground as if she were nothing more than a dead animal.

No part of the confession had surprised me much, but
seeing it all down in black-on-yellow, in Harmon Crane's own
words, had deepened my own depression. I got up from the
table and opened a can of Miller Lite and carried it into the
front room. Patches of fog were still swirling over this part of
the city; I stood in the bay window, watching the clash of blue

and gray overhead and thinking of how Kiskadon would react if he read those pages. Well, he *wasn't* going to read them, not if I could help it. He had fired me this morning; I no longer had an obligation to share my findings with him.

My findings. What was I doing here this afternoon, anyway, rummaging through all those old papers, fueling my rotten mood by wallowing in a poor dead writer's thirty-five-year-old weakness and torment? My job was done, for Christ's sake. I had been hired to find out why Crane killed himself, and I had found out, and I had been summarily fired for my efforts. And that was that.

Well, wasn't it?

Bertolucci's murder, I thought. Somebody killed him and the reason is linked to Harmon Crane and the hell with all this thinking. The job's not done yet and you know it. Quit maundering about it.

I finished the beer and went back into the kitchen and sat down at the table again. All right. Business correspondence. Letters from his agent informing him of acceptance of novels and short stories, of subsidiary rights sales on the Johnny Axe series. Other letters from the agent suggesting slick magazine story ideas or offering market tips. Letters from editors asking for revisions on this or that project. A two-page rejection letter detailing the reasons why a pulp editor was returning a story, across the first page of which Crane had scrawled the word *Bullshit!* Carbons of Crane's responses to some of the above. Carbons of cover letters sent with manuscript submissions to his agent and to various editors. Other business letters discussing financial matters with his agent, or making a specific point in rebuttal to an editorial request for revision; the latter were often phrased satirically, to take the sting out of the words: "Johnny Axe would *never* shoot an unarmed man, Mr. E., no matter that the unarmed man in this case is a 7-foot-tall Hindu snake charmer bent on remolding the shape of Johnny's spine. I have it on good authority that Mr. A. would not even shoot the *snake* unless it were packing a loaded gat."

Nothing for me there; I went on to the personal letters addressed to Crane, those dated the last few months of 1949. Fan mail, most of them, including a note on baby blue stationery from a woman in Michigan who said she had had "a wickedly erotic dream about dear Johnny Axe" and wondered if Mr. Crane ever passed through East Lansing on his way to and from New York because she'd *love* to meet him. Nothing from Kate Bertolucci. Nothing from Angelo Bertolucci. A scribbled note from Russ Dancer, suggesting a possible collaborative story idea; Crane had written at the bottom: "Come on Russ—trite!" A fannish note from Stephen Porter, telling Crane how much he'd enjoyed *Axe of Mercy*. Nothing from anyone else whose name I was familiar with.

Which left me with the carbons of personal letters Crane himself had written. The bulk of these were responses to fan letters, including a polite but unencouraging note to the lady in East Lansing. Letters to Russ Dancer and a couple of other writers, most of which were both humorous and scatological in tone; none of these was dated later than September of 1949. Only a few bore a post–October 15 date, and among those was a personal note dated December 7, Pearl Harbor Day:

> Dear L:
>   This is a difficult letter to write. Doubly so because I can't think straight these days (yes, I know the booze only makes it worse). But there's no one else I can turn to.
>   You know how I feel about Mandy. She's more important to me than anything else. If anything happens to me I want you to see to it she's cared for, financially and every other way. Can I count on you to do that?
>   The fact is, I can't go on much longer. I can't sleep, I can't eat, I can't work. Sometimes I think I'm close to losing my mind. There is too much festering inside me that I can't talk about, to you or to anyone

*else. No one must ever know the truth, least of all
Mandy. It would hurt her too much.*

*Life terrifies me more than death, yet I've been
too much of a coward to put an end to it. At least I
have been up to now. Soon I may find the strength.
Or perhaps circumstances will take it out of my
hands. In any case I will be better off dead, free of all
this pain. And Mandy will be better off without me,
even though she will never understand why.*

*As Johnny might say, I axe no mercy and I seek
no help. There is no mercy or help for me. I know
what I am. I ask only your word that you will take
care of Mandy.*

That was all. If he'd had anything else to say, it had gone
into a postscript on the original.

I read the carbon again, then a third time. Further proof
that Crane had been contemplating suicide for some time before December 10; that his mind had deteriorated to the point
where death was the only answer. A little rambling toward
the end: his mental state combined with the alcohol. Otherwise, coherent enough. Nothing unintelligible about it, nothing off-key.

Yet it struck an odd note for me, and I couldn't figure
out why.

Mandy was Amanda, of course. But who was L? Why
was he or she the only one Crane felt he could turn to about
his wife? I knew of no one close to Crane whose first or last
name began with the letter L. A nickname?

Maybe Porter would know. I went into the bedroom and
rang up his studio and got him on the line. And he said, "L?
No, I can't think of anyone at all. Certainly none of Harmon's
intimates had a name beginning with that letter."

Back into the kitchen to reread the carbon. That same
odd note . . . but why? Why?

The answer continued to elude me, even after three more
readings. Put it aside for now, I thought, come back to it

later. I paper-clipped it to Crane's fictionalized confession and left those sheets on the table. The rest of the stuff I put back into the cardboard box. Then I got another beer out of the refrigerator and went to call Kerry.

I needed some cheering up—bad.

She came over and cheered me up. A little while later I thought about rereading the carbon another time, but I didn't do it; I didn't want to get depressed all over again. Instead I reached for Kerry and suggested she cheer me up some more.

"Sex maniac," she said.

"Damn right," I said.

I cheered her up, too, this time.

At nine-thirty that night the telephone rang. Kerry and I were back in bed, watching an intellectual film—*Godzilla vs. Mothra*—on the tube. I caught up the receiver and said hello, and Wanda the Footwear Queen said, "You know who this is?" in a voice so slurred I could barely understand the words. Drunk as a barfly—the kind of drunk that teeters on the line between weepy and nasty.

"Uh-huh," I said.

"Juss want you know I hate your guts. Hers too, lil miss two fried eggs. Both your guts."

"Listen, why don't you go sleep it off—"

"Whyn't *you* go fuck yourself, huh?" she said, and I sighed and hung up on her.

"Who was that?" Kerry asked.

"The voice of unreason," I said.

And I thought: Poor Eberhardt. Poor, blind, stupid Eberhardt.

NINETEEN

S unday.

Kerry and I went downtown to the St. Francis Hotel for an early brunch, something we do occasionally. Afterward she suggested a drive down the coast and I said okay; the fog and high overcast had blown inland during the night, making the day clear and bright, if still windy. But I wasn't in much of a mood for that kind of Sunday outing. Not depressed so much today as restless—what a Texan I had known in the Army called a "daunciness"; I couldn't seem to relax, I couldn't seem to keep my mind off Harmon Crane and Michael Kiskadon and that damned letter carbon addressed to somebody with the initial L.

As perceptive as she is, Kerry read my mood and understood it. We were in Pacifica, following Highway One along the edge of the ocean, when she said, "Why don't we go back?"

"What?"

"Back home. You're not enjoying yourself and neither am I. You can drop me at my place if you'd rather be alone."

"Uh-uh. We'll go back, but I don't want to be alone. I'll only brood."

"You're doing that now."

"I'll do it worse if you're not around."

It was noon when we got back to the city. I drove to Pacific Heights—doing it automatically, without consulting Kerry. But she didn't seem to mind. Inside my flat, she went to make us some fresh coffee and I sat down with the box of Harmon Crane's papers. I reread the letter carbon. I reread the fictionalized confession. I reread the carbon one more time.

I was still bothered. And I still didn't know why.

Kerry had brought me some coffee and was sitting on the couch, reading one of my pulps. I said to her, "Let's play some gin rummy."

She looked up. "Are you sure that's what you want to do?"

"Sure I'm sure. Why?"

"You get grumpy when you lose at gin."

"Who says I'm going to lose?"

"You always lose when you're in a mood like this. You don't concentrate and you misplay your cards."

"Is that so? Get the cards."

"I'm telling you, you'll lose."

"Get the cards. I'm not going to lose."

She got the cards, and we played five hands and I lost every one because I couldn't concentrate and misplayed my cards. I *hate* it when she's right. I lost the sixth hand, too: she caught me with close to seventy points—goddamn face cards, I never had learned not to hoard face cards.

"You're a hundred and thirty-seven points down already," she said. "You want to quit?"

"Shut up and deal," I said grumpily.

And the telephone rang.

"Now who the hell is that?"

"Why don't you answer it and find out?"

"Oh, you're a riot, Alice," I said, which was a Jackie Gleason line from the old "Honeymooners" TV show. But she didn't get it. She said, "Who's Alice?" The telephone kept on ringing; I said, "One of these days, Alice, bang, zoom, straight to the moon," and got up and went into the bedroom to answer it.

A woman's voice made an odd chattering sound: "Muh-muh-muh," like an engine that kept turning over but wouldn't catch. But it wasn't funny; there was a familiar whining note of despair in the voice.

"Mrs. Kiskadon? What's the matter?"

She made the sound again, as if there were a liquidy blockage in her throat and she couldn't push the words past it. I told her to calm down, take a couple of deep breaths. I heard her do that; then she made a different noise, a kind of

166

strangled gulping, that broke the blockage and let the words come spilling out.

"It's Michael . . . you've got to help me, please, I don't know what to do!"

"What about Michael?"

"He said . . . he said he was going to kill himself. . . ."

I could feel the tension come into me, like air filling and expanding a balloon. "When was this?"

"A little while ago. He locked himself in his den last night after that Marin policeman left, he wouldn't come out, he sat in there all night doing God knows what. But this afternoon . . . he came out this afternoon and he had that gun in his hand, he was just carrying it in his hand, and he said . . . he . . ."

"Easy. Did you call his doctor?"

"No, I didn't think . . . I was too upset. . . ."

"Have you called anyone else?"

"No. Just you . . . you were the only person I could think of."

"All right. Is your husband in his den now?"

"I don't know," she said, "I'm not home."

"Not home? Where are you?"

"I couldn't stay there, I just . . . I couldn't, I had to get *out* of there. . . ."

"Where are you?" I asked her again.

"A service station. On Van Ness."

"How long have you been away from your house?"

"I don't know, not long. . . ."

"Listen to me. What did your husband say before you left? Tell me his exact words."

"He said . . . I don't *remember* his exact words, it was something about shooting himself the way his father did, like father like son, it was crazy talk. . . ."

"Did he *sound* crazy? Incoherent?"

"No. He was calm, that awful calm."

"Did he say anything else?"

167

"No, no, nothing."

"What did he do?"

"Went back into the den and locked the door."

"And then you left?"

"Yes. I told you, I couldn't stay there. . . ."

"How soon did you leave?"

"Right away. A minute or two."

"So it hasn't been more than fifteen or twenty minutes since he made his threat. He's probably all right; there's no reason to panic. You go back home and try to reason with him. Meanwhile, I'll call his doctor for you—"

"No," she said, "I can't go back there alone. Not alone. If you come . . . I'll meet you there. . . ."

"There's nothing I can do—"

"Please," she said, "I'll go home now, I'll wait for you."

"Mrs. Kiskadon, I think you—"

But there was a clicking sound and she was gone.

I put the handset back into its cradle. And left it there: I couldn't call Kiskadon's doctor because I didn't know who he was; she hadn't given me time to ask his name.

When I turned around Kerry was standing in the bedroom doorway. She said, "What was that all about?"

"Kiskadon threatened to kill himself a while ago. His wife is pretty upset; she wants me to go over there."

"Do you think he meant it?"

"I hope not."

"But he might have."

"Yeah," I said, "he might have."

"Then what are you waiting for? Go, for God's sake."

I went.

The green Ford Escort was parked in the driveway when I got to Twelfth Avenue and Lynn Kiskadon was sitting stiffly behind the wheel. She didn't move as I pulled to the curb in front, or when I got out and went around behind the Ford and up along her side. She didn't seem to know I was there until I tapped lightly on the window; then she jerked, like somebody

coming out of a daze, and her head snapped around. Behind the glass her face had a frozen look, pale and haggard, the eyes staring with the same fixed emptiness as the stuffed rodents in Angelo Bertolucci's display cases.

I reached down and opened the door. She said, "I didn't think you were coming," in a voice that was too calm, too controlled. She was one breath this side of a scream and two breaths short of hysteria.

"Did you check on your husband, Mrs. Kiskadon?"

"No. I've been sitting here waiting."

"You should have gone in—"

"I can't go in there," she said.

"You have to."

"No. I can't go *in* there, don't you understand?"

"All right."

"You go. I'll wait here."

"You'll have to give me the key."

She pulled the one out of the ignition and handed me the leather case it was attached to. "The big silver one," she said. "You have to wiggle it to get it into the lock."

I left her, went around the Ford and over onto the porch. I had just put the house key into the latch when I heard the car door slam. I didn't turn; I finished unlocking the door and pushed it open and walked inside.

Silence, except for the distant hum of an appliance that was probably the refrigerator. I went into the living room by a couple of paces, half-turning so that I could look back at the doorway. Lynn Kiskadon appeared there, hesitated, then entered and shut the door behind her.

"I couldn't wait out there," she said. "I wanted to but I couldn't. It's cold in the car."

I didn't say anything. Instead I went through into the hallway and along it to the closed door to Kiskadon's den. There wasn't anything to hear when I put my ear up close to the panel and listened. I knocked, called Kiskadon's name, and then identified myself.

No answer from inside.

169

Lynn Kiskadon was standing behind me, close enough so that I could hear the irregular rhythm of her breathing. There was a knot in my stomach and another one in my throat; the palms of my hands felt greasy. I wiped the right one on my pantleg, reached out and turned the doorknob. Locked.

I bent to examine the lock. It was the push-button kind that allows you to secure the door from either side. I straightened and looked at Mrs. Kiskadon; her skin seemed even paler now, splotched in places so that it resembled the color of buttermilk. "He might not be in there," I said. "He might be somewhere else in the house. Or outside."

"No," she said. "He's in there."

"I'll look around anyway. You wait here."

"Yes. All right."

It took me three minutes to search the place and determine that Michael Kiskadon wasn't anywhere else on the premises or in the yard out back. The knots in my stomach and throat were bigger, tighter, when I came back into the hallway. Lynn Kiskadon hadn't moved. She was standing there staring at the door as if it were the gateway to hell.

I said, "No other way inside except this door?"

"No."

"What about the window?"

"You'd have to use a ladder from the yard."

"Do you have a ladder?"

"Yes, but it's not high enough. We always hire somebody to do the windows, you see. There's a man who comes around, a handyman . . . he has a very high ladder."

"Mrs. Kiskadon, the only way I can get in there is to break down the door. Do you want me to do that?"

"Yes."

"You're sure?"

"Yes. Go ahead, do it. Break it down."

I caught hold of the knob. And a thought came to me: This is the way it was thirty-five years ago, the night Harmon Crane died. I shook it away. One sharp bump of my shoulder against the panel told me it was a tight lock and that I wasn't

going to get in by using that method. I stepped back, used the wall behind me for leverage, and drove the sole of my shoe into the wood just above the latch. That did it. There was a splintering sound as the bolt tore loose from the jamb-plate, and the door wobbled inward.

This is the way it was that night thirty-five years ago. . . .

I stayed in the doorway, trying to shield Mrs. Kiskadon with my body. But she pushed at me from behind, hit me with her fist, came past me. When she saw what I saw at the opposite end she made a thin, keening noise. I caught hold of her, but she fought loose and did a stumbling about-face and tried to run away into the hall. She didn't get any farther than the doorway before both her voice and her legs gave out. She fell sideways into the jamb, hard enough so that her head made an audible smacking noise against the wood.

She was on her knees when I got to her, shaking her head and moaning. But she wasn't hurt and she wasn't hysterical; just disoriented. I picked her up without resistance and carried her into the living room and put her down on the couch. She stayed there, not looking at me, not looking at anything in the room. I waited a few seconds anyway, just to make sure, before I went back into the den.

Kiskadon lay slumped over the desk top, left arm outflung, right arm hanging down toward the floor; his right temple was a mess of blood and torn and blackened flesh. Looking at him, I didn't feel any physical reaction—nothing at all this time except for the pity, always that same terrible feeling of pity. Second gunshot corpse in three days, and this one not nearly as bad as Bertolucci's had been. Maybe that was it. An overload that had temporarily short-circuited me inside.

Harmon Crane's way out, I thought. Just like that night in 1949.

A phone sat undisturbed on the desk, but I didn't want to use that one if there was another in the house. I started away—and something on the floor to one side and slightly behind the desk caught my attention. It was a brown leather

handbag, overturned so that some of its contents had spilled out. I moved closer and leaned over to look at the items: comb, compact, lipstick, wallet. But no keys. From that position I could also see the weapon; it wasn't in Kiskadon's hand, it was all the way under the chair on the left side—a Smith & Wesson snub-nosed .38, the kind known as a belly gun.

The sick feeling started then: short-circuit back the other way. But it was a different kind of sickness, as much a product of the actions of the living as of the presence of the dead. I clamped my teeth together and swallowed to keep it down.

Suicide, I thought again. Like father, like son.

Only now I didn't believe it.

TWENTY

As if things weren't bad enough, Leo McFate was in charge of the Homicide team that responded to my call.

McFate and I didn't get along. We had had run-ins a time or two in the past, but not for the usual reasons that an abrasiveness develops between cops and private detectives. The thing was, McFate didn't think of himself as a cop; he thought of himself as a *temporary* cop on his merry way to Sacramento and a job with the attorney general's office. He had ambitions, yes he did. He dressed in tailored suits and fancy ties, he read all the right books, he spoke with precise grammar, diction, and enunciation, he went to all the important social functions, and he sucked up to politicians, newspaper columnists, and flakes off the upper crust. He also considered himself a devilish ladies' man, with special attention to those women from eighteen to eighty who had money, social status, and the Right Connections. He didn't like me because he

thought I was beneath him. I didn't like him because I knew he was an asshole.

He came breezing in with another inspector, one I didn't know named Dwiggins, gave me a flinty-eyed look, and demanded to know where the deceased was. That was the way he talked; sometimes it was very comical to listen to him, but this wasn't one of them. I took him to the den and showed him the deceased. "Please wait in the kitchen," he said, as if that was where I belonged. And when I didn't trot off fast enough to suit him he said, "Well? Do what I told you."

I wished Eberhardt were here; Eberhardt knew how to get under McFate's skin and deflate him. I hadn't figured out the knack yet. All I could think of was to tell him to take a handful of ground glass and pound it up his tailpipe. Instead I turned without saying anything and went into the kitchen. Antagonizing cops is a stupid thing for anyone to do, and that goes double if you happen to be a private investigator.

McFate kept me waiting fifteen minutes, most of which time I spent prowling the kitchen like a cat in a cage. Once I thought of going in to check on Mrs. Kiskadon, but I didn't do it; I did not want to see her until after I had talked to McFate, and not even then if I could avoid it. She was in the bedroom, or had been just before McFate's arrival. She had got up off the couch while I was telephoning and walked in there and laid down on the bed with the door open. The one time I'd looked in on her she had been lying on her back, stiff-bodied, eyes closed, hands stretched out tight against her sides, like an embalmed corpse that had been arranged for viewing.

I felt keyed up, twitchy. Lynn Kiskadon and her dead husband were on my mind, but other things were rumbling around in there too. Things that I was beginning to understand and things that didn't seem to want to jell yet. None of them was very pleasant, but then murder never is.

When McFate finally came in I didn't give him a chance to be supercilious. I said, "There are some things you ought to know," and proceeded to explain about Kiskadon and Har-

mon Crane and the rest of it. Then I told him what I suspected about Kiskadon's death. He'd have figured it out himself eventually—it was pretty obvious, really, once you had all the facts—but I didn't feel like waiting around for his wheels to start turning on their own initiative.

McFate looked at me the way an entomologist would look at a not very interesting bug. I looked right back at him, which was something I never enjoy doing. The son of a bitch is handsome on top of everything else: dark hair gray at the temples, precisely trimmed mustache, a cleft in his chin as big as a woman's navel. No wonder the ladies loved him—those of nondiscriminating taste, anyway. Hell, no wonder the *politicians* loved him.

He said, "You think it's a one-eight-seven? Why?"

One-eight-seven is police slang; Section 187 of the California Penal Code pertains to willful homicide. "I didn't say that," I said.

"If his wife killed him, it's a one-eight-seven."

"I know that. But I didn't say I think she killed him. I said I think she's covering up. She knew he was dead long before we found him."

"I repeat: Why?"

"Three reasons. First, her actions today, the things she said to me on the phone and after I got here—they don't ring true. She said she didn't call her husband's doctor because she was too upset. She didn't call the police either. And she didn't try to get a friend or a neighbor to help her. Instead she left the house, drove down to Van Ness, and called me. Why? Because she wanted someone who knew how suicidal he'd been to find the body; she didn't want to admit that he was dead *before* she left here."

"Hardly conclusive," McFate said.

I said, "Then there's the gun."

"What about the gun?"

"It's under Kiskadon's chair. You saw that. If he shot himself, how did it get all the way under there?"

"It fell out of his hand and bounced on the carpet,"

McFate said. "If you remember, his right arm is hanging down near the floor."

"Leo," I said, and watched him wince. He hates for me to call him Leo; he would prefer that I call him Mr. McFate, or maybe just sir. "Leo, the gun is lying all the way under the chair, over on the *left* side. Even if it fell out of his hand, it's not likely that it could bounce more than a foot on a shag carpet."

He scowled at me. "I suppose you deduce from that that Mrs. Kiskadon threw the weapon under the chair."

"She had something to do with it being there, yes. I can't say whether or not she threw it under the chair, or whether or not she actually shot him. But she was in the room when he died."

"And just how do you deduce *that?*"

"Her handbag, Leo. On the floor behind the desk with half its contents spilled out."

"I saw it," he said stiffly. "I assumed she dropped it when the two of you found the deceased."

"Uh-uh. She didn't have that bag or any other when I got here. Not in her car, not in her hand when she followed me in. She told me her husband had come out of the den earlier, waving the gun around, and then went back in there and locked the door; she didn't say *she'd* been in there, and she would have unless she had something to hide. And if she wasn't in the den, what was the purse doing in there? And why is it upended on the floor unless there was a struggle or something that led to the shooting?"

McFate didn't say anything. But he was thinking about it now. You didn't have to beat him over the head with logic—not too hard, anyhow.

"The car keys must have been in her coat pocket," I said. "Either that, or she scooped them up off the floor before she ran out. I guess you noticed that the door has a push-button lock. Kiskadon probably pushed the button when he went in there for the last time; all she did was shut the door on her

way out, maybe without even realizing it. All she was interested in was getting away from here."

McFate said grudgingly, "If you're right, then she must have murdered him."

"Not necessarily. It could have been an accident—a struggle over the gun. Why don't you ask her?"

"I don't need you to tell me my job."

"God forfend I should ever try."

"Wait here," he said, and stalked out.

I waited, but not for long. I was even twitchier now and the kitchen seemed too small and too much of a reminder of the life the Kiskadons had shared before today, when what they shared became death. People were moving around out in the hall; I opened the door and looked out. The assistant coroner had arrived and Dwiggins was ushering him into the den. I came out of the kitchen and wandered down there, being careful not to get in anybody's way.

At an angle I could see part of the room, but not the part where the body lay. One of the lab men was down on his knees, poking among the splinters of wood that my forced entry had torn from the jamb. I watched him—and the thought came to me again that this was the way it had been thirty-five years ago, on the night Harmon Crane died. Man is shot in a locked office, door gets busted in, the cops come and poke around and clean up the remains. Some things don't change in thirty-five years; some things never change.

And who says lightning doesn't strike twice? It had struck twice in this case, one father and one son all those years apart, one suicide and one manslaughter. . . .

Twice, I thought.

Or *was* it one of each? Kiskadon's death had looked like a suicide but wasn't. Why not the same with Harmon Crane? Even with that locked door, the door that the police back then had said couldn't have been gimmicked—wasn't it possible Crane had been murdered after all?

Twice, I thought. Twice!

And I had it. At first, just the simple misdirection gim-

mick that had fooled the police and everyone else in 1949. But once I had that much, I began to see the rest of it, too: the distortions and subterfuge and misconceptions that had befuddled me, the full circumstances of Crane's death, the significance of that letter carbon, the probable reason Angelo Bertolucci had died and the name of the person who had murdered him. All of it exposed at last, dark and ugly, like those mildewing bones out on the rim of Tomales Bay.

I considered telling it to McFate, but that would have been like telling it to the wall. Besides, it wasn't his case; it was only peripherally related to Kiskadon's death. DeKalb was the man I wanted to tell it to. But not yet, not until I got some personal satisfaction first.

Before long McFate reappeared. I was still in the hallway, still twitchy because I wanted to be on my way. He showed me his scowl and said, "I thought I told you to wait in the kitchen."

"I had to go to the toilet. What did Mrs. Kiskadon say?"

". . . You were right," he said in reluctant tones. He was looking, now, at the top button on my jacket. "She admitted it."

"I thought she might. She isn't a very good liar."

"No, she isn't."

"She didn't murder him, did she?"

"An accident, she claims."

"It probably was," I said. "She's not the type to commit premeditated homicide."

McFate said with heavy sarcasm, "Thank you for your expert opinion."

"You're welcome. How did it happen?"

"Her husband spent the night in his den, just as she told you. She tried to talk him out this morning but he wouldn't come, not until about noon."

"And he was waving the gun around when he finally showed."

"Yes. He threatened to shoot himself and she told him to go ahead, she couldn't stand it any longer. Fed up, as she put

177

it. He reentered the den and she followed him. She'd been about to go for a drive, just to get away for a while, which is why she was carrying her handbag."

"Uh-huh."

"Kiskadon sat at his desk. She tried to reason with him, but he wouldn't listen; he put the weapon to his temple and held it there with his finger on the trigger, saying he intended to fire."

"Uh-huh," I said again. "At which point she panicked and tried to take it away from him. They struggled, she dropped her handbag, and the gun went off."

"So she alleges."

"How did the gun get under his chair?"

"It fell on the desk after the discharge," McFate said. "She must have swept it off onto the floor; she doesn't remember that part of it very clearly."

I nodded. "Poor Kiskadon. If she'd left him alone, he probably wouldn't have gone through with it. Suicides don't make a production number out of what they're going to do, usually; they just do it."

"Really? You're an accredited psychologist as well as an expert in criminal behavior, I suppose."

"If you say so, Leo."

The scowl again. "I don't like you, you know that?"

"That's too bad. I think *you're* the cat's nuts."

"Are you trying to insult me?"

"Me? Heavens no. How's Mrs. Kiskadon?"

"Weepy," McFate said, and grimaced. He didn't like women to be weepy; he liked them to be a) cooperative, b) generous, and c) naked. "Dwiggins is calling a matron and her doctor."

"Are you going to book her?"

"Certainly."

"You could go a little easy on her. She's no saint, but she has had a rough time of it."

"You're trying to tell me my job again. I don't like that."

"Sorry. Is it all right if I leave now?"

"You'll have to sign a statement."

"I can do that later, down at the Hall."

"What's your hurry? You seem impatient."

"There's somebody I have to see."

"Oh? And who would that be?"

"A lady friend. You can understand that, can't you?"

"The redhead I met once? What's her name?"

"Kerry Wade. Yes."

"Attractive woman. I can't imagine what she sees in you."

"Neither can I. Look, Leo; can I leave or not?"

"Leave. I'm tired of looking at you." His superciliousness was back; he had resumed control of things. "Give my regards to Ms. Wade."

"I'll do that," I said. "She thinks you're the cat's nuts, too."

But it wasn't Kerry I was planning to see. It was Thomas J. Yankowski, the retired shyster, the prize son of a bitch.

Yank-'Em-Out Yankowski—murderer.

TWENTY-ONE

There was nobody home at Yankowski's house except for the snarling brute that guarded the place. It came flying at the sound of the bell, just as it had the first time I'd been here, and slammed into the door and then stood there growling its fool head off. I went back up the stairs and over to the street-level garage door and peered through the mail slot. Dark-shadowed emptiness looked back at me from within.

But if I could help it I wasn't going to go away from here empty-handed. I set out to canvass the neighbors, and I would have tried every house in this section of St. Francis Wood if it

had been necessary. But it wasn't. The second one I went to, diagonally across the street from Yankowski's, produced just the kind of occupant I was looking for: a fat woman in her fifties, with hennaed hair and rouged cheeks, who reminded other people's business along with her own and who didn't mind talking about it.

"Well, no, I *don't* know where Mr. Yankowski went today. Not *exactly*, that is." She was also the type who speaks in italics; emphasis was very important to her, so you'd be sure to take her meaning. "But he *might* be out at Fort Funston."

"Oh?"

"Yes. I happen to know he goes there on weekends. He likes to watch those young people with their gliders. *Hang* gliders, they call them. That's a very dangerous sport, don't you think? Hang gliding?"

"Yes, ma'am."

"He likes to walk along the cliffs too, Mr. Yankowski does. He's quite spry for a man of his years. I wish my *husband* were half so energetic—"

"Excuse me, ma'am. Can you tell me what kind of car Mr. Yankowski drives?"

"Car? Why, it's a Cadillac. Yes, *definitely* a Cadillac."

"Black, isn't it?"

"Oh yes. Black as a nigger's bottom," she said, and gave me a perfectly guileless smile.

I went away from her without another word.

Fort Funston is at the far southwestern edge of the city, off Skyline Boulevard above and beyond Lake Merced—a fifteen-minute drive from St. Francis Wood. There isn't much there except for the launching and landing area for hang-glider enthusiasts and close to a mile of footpaths along the cliffs overlooking the sea. One of the more scenic but under-visited sections of the Golden Gate National Recreation Area.

It was after five when I rolled in there, less than an hour before sunset, and only a scattering of cars was still parked in

the big lot. The only people I saw were a trio of muscular young guys furling a glider and tying it to a rack across the top of an old Mustang. I spotted the black Cadillac immediately, parked over by the restrooms—the only one in the lot. I pulled in alongside it and got out and looked at the license plate. One of the personalized ones: MR TJY. Yankowski's, all right. I went around to examine the driver's side.

Unscratched, undented. And gleaming with what had to be new paint. The whole damn *car* had been repainted.

He was a shrewd bastard, Mr. TJY. He'd had bodywork done on the Caddy right away, followed by the brand-new paint job, and I should have known that was what he'd do. Hide anything that might be incriminating and hide it quick. And no ordinary body shop—the type that keeps records and cooperates with the police—to do the work, either. He'd been a shyster for too many years not to pick up the name of somebody who would do repair work, sanding, and painting on the QT, for the right price.

And there, goddamn it, went the only solid piece of evidence linking Yankowski to the murder of Angelo Bertolucci.

I moved away from the Caddy, over to the main asphalt path that led out onto the cliffs. Sunset Trail, they called it, and it was an apt name: the sunset starting on the horizon now, in deep golds streaked with red, was quite a sight from up here. Just as impressive, from farther along, was the view you had of Ocean Beach all the way to the Cliff House in the hazy distance. Not so impressive, lying closer in, were the offshore dredgers and the long finger of the pipeline pier that were part of an endless city sewage project.

Irregular sandy paths branched off the main path, meandering through dark red and brown and green iceplant to the rim of the cliffs. A few people were out there, one of them with an easel set up, painting the sunset; none of them was old enough to be Yankowski. I stayed on Sunset Trail. I have a thing about heights, and the dropoff over there was sheer and at least two hundred feet to the strip of beach below.

Benches were strung out at intervals along the trail, and

on one of them a fifth of a mile from the parking lot I found Yankowski. He was sitting there alone, nobody else within a hundred yards, watching the quicksilver shimmer of the dying sun on the water. The wind was strong and turning cold and I wasn't dressed warmly enough; goosebumps had spread up my arms and across my shoulders. But old Yank-'Em-Out was bundled up in a heavy mackinaw and gloves and a Scottish cap, and he looked as relaxed and comfortable as he had the day I'd talked to him in his own back yard.

He didn't pay any attention to me until I stopped in front of him, blocking his view, and said, "Hello, Yankowski."

His frown was full of displeasure. "You again. I thought I told you I didn't want anything more to do with you."

"Yes? Well, you're going to have plenty more to do with me, Counselor. Starting right now."

"I am not," he said, and he got up and pushed past me and started back along Sunset Trail. At first I thought he was going to stay on it, which would have made bracing him easier for me; instead he veered off onto one of the sandy paths toward the cliff edge. I hesitated—I just don't like heights— but I went after him anyway, skirting scrub bushes and passing over tiny dunes like faceless heads with iceplant for hair.

Yankowski stopped a few feet from the edge, where the ground rose a little and then fell away sharply into an eroded declivity. I stopped too, but a couple of steps farther back and at an angle to him. Still, I was close enough to the edge so that I could look down part of the cliff face, see the surf licking at the beach far away at the bottom. The gooseflesh rippled on my arms and shoulders, a sensation that had nothing to do with the wind or the cold.

"Yankowski."

He turned. "Damn you, go away. Leave me alone."

"No. You're going to talk to me."

"Why should I?"

"Because I know you killed Angelo Bertolucci," I said. "And I know why."

He had a good poker face, from all his years in court, but

he couldn't keep his body from stiffening. His gloved hands hooked into fists—and then relaxed. He watched me silently out of dark, cold eyes that had no fear in them, only wariness and an animal cunning.

I said, "Well? Do we talk?"

"You talk," he said. "I'll listen."

"Sure, why not. I've got the whole thing figured out, starting with Harmon Crane. I'll tell you the way I think it was; you tell me if I'm right."

He pursed his lips and said nothing. Past him, the fiery rim of the sun was just fusing with the ocean; the swath it laid across the water was turning from silver to gold.

I said, "All right. Crane liked to get away from the city from time to time, to be alone for a week or two; he worked better that way. He liked the isolation of Tomales Bay and he rented a cabin up there from Angelo Bertolucci. Bertolucci didn't like Crane much, but he liked Crane's money. What Crane liked was Bertolucci's wife, Kate.

"I don't know how long he and Kate Bertolucci had been seeing each other, when or how it started. Doesn't matter. Doesn't matter either that they both had reasons for turning to each other, or what those reasons were. What's important is that they had an affair, and that Bertolucci found out about it.

"Bertolucci went to the cabin one day in late October of 1949, probably with the idea of catching his wife and Crane together. But she was there alone; Crane had gone to buy groceries. There was an argument; Bertolucci lost his head and clubbed her to death with a piece of stovewood. Then panic set in and he ran.

"Crane came back and found the body and *he* panicked. Instead of notifying the county sheriff, he cleaned up the blood and buried Kate's body in a fissure opened by an earthquake the day before. After which he packed up and beat it back to San Francisco. But the whole ugly business was too much for his conscience. Guilt began to eat at him. And paranoia: he was afraid Bertolucci might decide to come after *him*

183

too. He started hitting the bottle; he didn't have the guts to do anything else, including confront Bertolucci.

"Six weeks or so went by and nothing happened except that Crane's mental condition kept getting wrose. He thought about killing himself but he didn't have the guts for that either, not quite. He almost wished Bertolucci would come and do it for him."

I paused. "How am I doing so far, Yankowski?"

He stayed silent, unmoving. His eyes were small and black under the bill of his cap—little poison-drops of hate.

"So then came the night of December tenth," I said, "and Crane's death. But it wasn't suicide, the way everybody thought—the way I thought myself until this morning. That locked office was what threw all of us. The police had ruled out any gimmick work with the door and windows; it had to be suicide. Only it wasn't, it was murder."

Yankowski said, "And I suppose you think I murdered him."

"No. I think Bertolucci murdered him, just as Crane was afraid he might. And I think you covered it up for Bertolucci by making it look like a suicide."

"Now why would I do that?"

"Because you were in love with Amanda Crane and you didn't want Crane's affair and the rest of it to come out; you knew she was the fragile type and you were afraid of what the scandal might do to her. But you miscalculated, Yankowski. You did it all for nothing. Her mind wasn't even strong enough to withstand a suicide; she cracked up and never recovered. And you, the big Prince Charming, you abandoned her. You weren't about to saddle yourself with half a woman who needed constant care—not a fast-rising young shyster like you."

He said between his teeth, "You son of a bitch."

"Me? That's a laugh, coming from one as nasty as you."

His hands fisted again. He seemed to lean forward a little, shifting his weight. The hate in his eyes was as cold and black as death.

"Go ahead," I said, "try it. But *you'll* be the one who goes over the edge, not me. I've got forty pounds and fifteen years on you."

The tension stayed in him a couple of seconds longer; he glanced away from me, down the sandy cut to the cliff wall and the beach far below. Then he relaxed, not slowly but all at once. He liked living, Yank-'Em-Out did, and he wanted to hang onto the time he had left. I watched him regroup. You could almost see the internal shifting of gears, almost hear the click and whir of the shrewd little computer inside his head.

Pretty soon he said, "You think you know what happened at Crane's house that night? Go ahead, tell me."

I relaxed a little too, but I stayed wary. And I kept my feet spread and planted on the firmer footing of the iceplant. I said, "To begin with, Crane didn't telephone you and ask you to come to his house; it was the other way around. You went to see him at *your* initiative."

"Did I? Why?"

"Because he sent you a letter asking you to take care of Amanda if anything happened to him; he either knew or suspected how you felt about her. The letter mentioned suicide, too—he must have worked himself up to the point where he figured he could finally do it—and also hinted that he had a deep dark secret he couldn't tell anyone, least of all his wife. You're not the type to let a challenge like that go by. You went to his place to try to pry it out of him."

"How do you know about this alleged letter?"

"Crane kept a carbon of it. I found it among some papers of his."

"You claim it was addressed to me? That it has my name on it?"

I didn't lie to him; if his memory was good enough, he knew better. I didn't say anything. But I was certain that the letter *had* been addressed to him; once the rest of it came clear, so had the meaning of the "Dear L" salutation. "L" wasn't the first letter of somebody's name. It was the first letter of Yankowski's profession. Dear L: Dear Lawyer.

Yankowski said, "It makes no difference either way. If such a letter exists, I submit it contains nothing incriminating to me and I deny ever receiving it."

"We'll see what the law has to say about that."

"The law," he said. Contempt bracketed the words. "Don't talk about the law to *me*, detective. The law is a tool, to be used and manipulated by those who understand it."

"What a sweet bastard you are."

We watched each other—the two old pit bulls, one of us with the stain of blood on his muzzle. The wind gusted, swirling particles of sand that stung my cheek. Out to sea, the bottom quarter of the sun had slid below the horizon. The surface in front of it looked as if it were on fire, the dredgers close to shore as if they were burned-out hulks that the flames had consumed before moving on.

"You want to hear the rest of it?" I said at length. "Just to prove to you I know what I'm talking about?"

"Go ahead. Talk. I'm listening."

"Bertolucci also picked the night of December tenth to pay a visit to Crane. Maybe he'd been watching the house; that would explain how he knew Crane was alone. He might have gone there with the intention of murdering Crane; he might only have wanted to talk to him, find out what he'd done with Kate's body. Still, he had to've taken the *potential* for another murder along with him. I figure that's one of the reasons he waited so long. He was scared and confused and no mental giant besides; it took time to nerve himself up.

"So Bertolucci went into the house. Probably walked right in; I was told Crane never locked the front door. He found Crane in his office, drunk as usual, trying to work up the last bit of nerve he needed to shoot himself; that twenty-two of his must have been out in plain sight. As drunk as Crane was, as much as he wanted to die, maybe he invited Bertolucci to shoot him, get it over with. Or maybe it was Bertolucci's idea when he saw the twenty-two. In any case Bertolucci had gotten away with his wife's murder up to then and he wanted to keep on getting away with it. So he used

that twenty-two—put it up against the side of Crane's head and pulled the trigger.

"Enter Thomas J. Yankowski, servant of the people. Bertolucci might have shot you too; I wish to Christ he had. But it must have taken all his nerve to do the job on Crane. You got him calmed down, you got the full story out of him, you got him to trust you. Easy pickings for a glib young shyster. You told him you'd help him, gave him some kind of song and dance, then sent him on his way. And when he was gone you rigged the murder to look like suicide."

"Fascinating," he said. "How did I accomplish that?"

"Oh, you were smart. You didn't try anything fancy; you came up with a method so simple and clever everybody overlooked it. Until now. Until Michael Kiskadon got himself shot and killed in his den earlier today, under circumstances similar to what happened to his father. You didn't know about that, did you? Kiskadon's death?"

Yankowski was silent again.

"The first thing you did when you were alone with Crane's body that night was to type out the suicide note on his machine. But you wanted the phrasing to be just right— Crane's style, Crane's words, not yours. You'd brought along his letter to you and you realized that if you excerpted parts of it, it would make a perfect suicide note. So that's what you did: lifted sentences and partial sentences right out of the letter, changing nothing but the tenses here and there.

"I saw the text of the suicide note in the old newspaper accounts, early in the week. When I read the letter carbon something about it struck me as odd, but I couldn't put my finger on it until this morning, after I found Kiskadon. Then it came to me how similar the letter was to the suicide note, phrases like 'life terrifies me more than death.' Crane was in no shape that night to plagiarize himself, either consciously or unconsciously—not exact wording in the exact order he'd used in his letter to you. Somebody else *had* to have typed the suicide note. And that somebody had to be you."

"Why did it have to be me?"

"Because there's only one way the cover-up gimmick could have been worked, and the only man who could have worked it is the one who broke into the office later on, in the presence of Amanda Crane. You, Yankowski. Couldn't have been Adam Porter; his brother told me Adam was frail and frail men don't go busting in doors, not when there's a healthy young buck like you around. *You* broke into Crane's office that night. And not once—twice.

"That's the explanation in one word: twice. After you typed the suicide note you went out into the hall, shut the door behind you, locked it with the key, and broke it in so that there'd be evidence of forced entry. Then you put the key in the lock on the *inside* and shut the door again. No one could tell from the hallway that it had been forced.

"You left the house then, making sure you weren't seen, and waited around outside somewhere until Porter and Amanda returned home from dinner. At which point you pretended to have just arrived. When the three of you went upstairs to Crane's office, you grabbed the doorknob and pretended it was locked. 'We'd better break in,' you said. You threw your weight against the door, holding tight to the knob to provide some noise and resistance, and then let go and the door popped open. Porter and Amanda were too upset to notice anything amiss; and besides, there was plenty of evidence that there *had* been a forced entry. You also had Porter to verify to the police that the door was forced in his presence and that the key was in the lock on the inside."

Yankowski still didn't have anything to say. He looked away from me again, out to where a freighter, like a two-dimensional silhouette, seemed about to be engulfed by the shimmery fire on the horizon. The wind was even colder now. Distantly a foghorn sounded, spreading the news that fog-banks were lying out there somewhere and might soon be blowing in.

I said, "For thirty-five years you got away with it, you and Bertolucci. Ancient history, half-forgotten, and the two of you probably long out of touch. But then Kiskadon showed

up. And I showed up. You weren't worried at first; you didn't figure I could dig deep enough after all that time to get at the truth. But my bet is you hunted up Bertolucci just the same, first to determine if he was still alive and then to warn him about me.

"My visit to Bertolucci on Wednesday didn't seem to unnerve him much; but when I found his wife's bones that same day—he read about it in the papers or heard about it somehow on Thursday—he got nervous and called you. You went up there to see him. With the intention of killing him to keep him quiet? No, probably not. But something happened when you got to his house, an argument of some kind: he was a crazy old coot and you're a mean bugger when you lose your temper. He probably waved that shotgun at you, and you took it away from him and let fly with both barrels.

"You didn't find out until later that it was my car you ran into when you were tearing out of there. If you needed any more reason to have the damage to your car fixed, that was it. Nice repair work, too; nice new paint job. But the authorities will find out who did the work for you."

"I doubt that," Yankowski said.

"Even if they don't, there'll be something else to tie you to Bertolucci and the murder."

"I also doubt that," he said, "since everything you've said is an outrageous tall tale." He seemed to have relaxed completely, to have regained his arrogant manner. The hate was still in his eyes, but it was shaded now by a thin veil of amusement. He took out one of his fat green cigars, turned his back to the wind, and managed to get the cigar fired with a gold butane lighter. When he faced me again he said, "You don't have a shred of proof to back up any of your allegations and you know it. You can't prove that I conspired with Angelo Bertolucci to cover up a murder in 1949. A letter addressed to me that happens to resemble Harmon Crane's suicide note is hardly evidence of any wrongdoing on my part. The police were satisfied that Crane's death was suicide; you have no legal grounds for reopening the case after all these

years. You have no proof that I ever even met this man Bertolucci. You have no eyewitnesses who can identify me as being in or near his home on the night of his death. You have no physical evidence of any kind against me. You have nothing, in short, except a great deal of fanciful speculation. Fiction, not fact."

"That isn't going to stop me from taking it to the authorities," I said.

"Do as you like. But I warn you, detective. I'd like nothing better than to instigate a lawsuit against you for harassment and defamation of character."

"And I warn *you*, Yankowski, you won't get away with it this time. Not this time."

He smiled at me mirthlessly around his cigar. "Won't I?" he said, and turned his back—a gesture of contempt and dismissal—and walked a short distance away. Stood there smoking and looking out to sea, with his back still turned.

Frustration was sharp in me; he was right and I knew it, and I hated him, too, in that moment, as much as I have ever hated any man for his corruption. The hatred brought on an irrational impulse to go over and give him a push, one little push that would send him hurtling to his death. Immediately I swung around and went the other way, back through the sand and iceplant to Sunset Trail and along it to the parking lot.

I could never have done it, of course—pushed him off that cliff, killed him in cold blood. It would have made me just like him, it would have turned my soul to slime. No, I could never have done it.

But on the long drive home, thinking about him standing up there so smug and sure, so goddamn *safe*, I almost wished I had.

TWENTY-TWO

I did not call Sergeant DeKalb that night, although I considered it. What I had to say to him, the full story of Yankowski's guilt, was better dealt with in person. It could wait until the morning.

On Monday, before I drove up to San Rafael to see him, I stopped by the office to find out if there had been any weekend calls. And damned if Eberhardt wasn't already there, even though it was only ten past nine—making coffee and cussing the hot plate because it was taking too long to get hot.

"Surprise," I said as I shut the door. "The prodigal has returned."

"What the hell does that mean?"

"You haven't been around the past few days."

"Yeah, well, I took a long weekend. So what?"

"So nothing. But a lot of things have been happening."

"So I read in the papers. You can't keep your ass out of homicide cases, can you? One of these days somebody's going to shoot it off for you."

"Or part of it. Then I can be as half-assed as you."

"Is that supposed to be funny?"

"No, I guess not."

"I don't feel very comical today," he said.

"Neither do I."

"Then don't try to be funny." He smacked the hot plate with the heel of his hand. "Frigging thing takes forever to get hot," he said.

"Any calls on the machine? Or didn't you check it?"

"I checked it. No calls."

"Figures." Leaving my coat on, I went over and cocked a hip against my desk. "Where'd you go for the weekend?" I asked him.

"Up to the Delta."

"Fishing?"

"Yeah."

"Wanda go with you?"

Pause. Then he said, "No."

"I kind of figured she didn't."

"Yeah? Why?"

"She called me up Saturday night."

"What for?"

"To tell me she hated my guts. Kerry's too."

"Drunk?"

"Sounded that way. Eb, listen . . ."

"Shut up," he said. He put his back to me and went to his desk and sat down. Out came one of his pipes and his tobacco pouch; he began loading up, getting flakes of the smelly black shag he used all over his blotter.

Neither of us said anything for a while; we just sat there, Eberhardt thumbing tobacco into his pipe as if he were crushing ants, me listening to the coffee water start to boil on the hot plate.

He said finally, "What else she say on the phone?"

"She told me to go fuck myself."

"Yeah," he said. "Anything else?"

"No. I hung up on her."

"Nothing about us, then. Her and me."

"No. What about the two of you?"

"We broke it off," he said.

"Broke it off? You mean your engagement?"

"The whole thing. It's finished between us. Kaput."

That threw me a little; it was the kind of surprise that usually comes only on birthdays and Christmas. I said, "When did this happen?"

"Tuesday night. Big goddamn battle. I haven't seen her since and I won't either."

"What was the battle about?"

"What do you think?" he said. "She kept bad-mouthing you and Kerry. Drinking vodka like it was water and ranting like a crazy woman. Kept saying she was gonna get back at the two of you. Do something drastic, she said. Talk to one of

her ex-husbands, get him to throw a scare into Kerry some night—shit like that."

"She'd better not go through with it."

"She won't. It was just crazy talk."

I said diplomatically, "Well, I guess she had a right to be upset."

"Upset, sure, but not out for blood. Not crazy. No damn right to act that way at all."

He defended us, I thought, Kerry and me. *That's* what the big blowup was all about.

"Made me look at her different," he said, "made me think maybe she wasn't the woman I figured she was. Made me compare her to Kerry, you want to know the truth." He looked away from me abruptly, out into the airshaft behind his desk. "Ahh," he said, "the hell with it. She's a bitch, that's all. I always did have a knack for picking bitches."

"Eb . . ."

"Look at Dana. First-class bitch."

Dana was his ex-wife and not nearly as bad as he tried to paint her. Maybe Wanda wasn't either—but I wouldn't have wanted to bet on it.

"Eb, why didn't you tell me this on Wednesday or Thursday?"

"Didn't feel like talking about it," he said. "I needed to get away for a few days, get her out of my system."

"And? She out of it now?"

"Not completely. But she will be. All I got to do is keep thinking about what she called me."

"What did she call you?"

"Never mind." He lit his pipe and puffed up enough smoke to make the office look and smell like a grass fire.

"Come on, Eb, what did she call you?"

"I said never mind. I don't want to talk about her anymore, all right?"

I let it drop. But a while later, as I was getting ready to leave for San Rafael, Eberhardt said out of the gray of his pipe smoke, "Tits aren't everything, for Christ's sake."

"What?"

"Tits. They're not everything."

"Uh, no, they're not."

"Man is attracted by more than that in a woman. Man looks for somebody he can be comfortable with, somebody he can *talk* to. You know what I mean?"

"Sure I do."

"She said I was a piss-poor excuse for a man because all I cared about were her tits. Said I was a baby—a tit wallower. How the hell do you like that?"

"The nerve of the woman," I said, straightfaced.

I managed to make it out of the door and over to the stairs before I burst out laughing.

Kerry laughed, too, when I told her about it that night. In fact, she thought "tit wallower" was the funniest expression she'd heard in *months*. She kept repeating it and then sailing off into whoops and snorts.

When she calmed down I said, "So now you're vindicated, lady."

"Vindicated?"

"The Great Spaghetti Assault. It was a damned stupid thing to do, but it got all the right results."

"Mmm," she said. Her eyes were bright with reminiscence; she really did hate Wanda a lot. "And I'd do it again, too, if I got drunk enough."

"I'll bet you would."

"For Eberhardt's sake."

"Right."

"God, what a relief she's out of his life. The idea of having to attend their wedding gave me nightmares. She probably would have worn white, too."

"Probably."

"And Eberhardt would have been in a tuxedo. He'd have looked like a big bird, I'll bet. A black-winged, white-breasted tit wallower," she said and off she went into more whoops and snorts.

I sighed and picked up her empty wineglass and went into the kitchen to refill it. We were in her apartment tonight, because the weather was still good and the view from her living room window is slightly spectacular on clear nights. When I came back she had herself under control again. "I'll be good," she said when I handed her the wine.

"Uh-huh."

"No, I will. I'll be serious. You're in a serious mood tonight, aren't you?"

"More or less."

"Michael Kiskadon?"

"Yeah. He's been on my mind all day."

"Have you heard anything more about his wife?"

"Some. I talked to Jack Logan at the Hall; she's still in custody, still holding up all right."

"Is the D.A. going to prosecute her?"

"Probably not. She didn't murder her husband; all she did was try to cover up her part in the accident. Any competent lawyer could get her off without half trying."

"Lawyers," Kerry said, and made a face.

"Yeah."

"Yankowski—what about him? *He's* not going to get off, is he?"

"That's the way it looks," I said. "DeKalb went to see him today, after we talked, and he didn't get any further than I did. The law can't touch him for what he did in 1949. And there's just no proof that he killed Bertolucci. Unless DeKalb can find out who did the repair work and paint job on his Cadillac, there's nothing at all to tie him and Bertolucci together."

Kerry seemed to have grown as sobersided as I felt. She scowled into her wineglass. "It's not right," she said. "He's a cold-blooded murderer. He *can't* get away with it."

"Can't he? A lot of things aren't right in the world these days, babe. Who says there has to be justice?"

"I'd like to believe there is."

"So would I," I said. "But I'm afraid there isn't."

EPILOGUE

Well, maybe there is. Sometimes.

Eight days later, at 6:20 in the evening, Thomas J. Yankowski suffered a fatal heart attack while watching the news on TV. He didn't die immediately; he died forty minutes later, in an ambulance on the way to Mission Emergency Hospital. He had a history of heart trouble—he'd had a mild attack a few years ago, as Eberhardt had mentioned to me—but I like to think the seizure was the direct result of the stress and strain of having committed one crime too many. I also like to think he was coherent during the last forty minutes of his life, that he believed the attack was punishment for his sins and perhaps he faced an even greater punishment to come.

Not that any of that matters, of course. What matters is the simple fact that he was dead, just as Kate Bertolucci and Harmon Crane and Angelo Bertolucci and Michael Kiskadon were dead; and now the pathetic little drama they had enacted was over. Ashes to ashes, dust to dust. A few insignificant bones scattered and lost in the graveyard of time.

It makes you wonder. Sometimes there is justice, yes. But does *that* matter, either, in the larger scheme of things—whatever that scheme may be?

Maybe it does.

Like love, like compassion and caring and friendship—maybe it does.

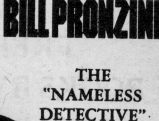